C000292031

To   Sian
Happy reading.

ISBN: 978-1-9999123-0-7

Chapter 1

Valermos dreamed of fairer days, of a love long since lost. When he woke, he barely registered the sound of sirens blaring around him. For a moment he still believed he was dreaming, lost in the bliss between fantasy and reality. He looked through the palace window at the artificial red sky of Jupiter, quickly realising that if he were still dreaming, what lay beyond was the stuff of nightmares.

He recognised the ships from the Earth Alliance broadcasts: they belonged to the Voltron; malicious automatons built to destroy whatever they touched at the behest of their deranged master. Their ships swarmed the horizon, descending on the marble-like city below him.

His people were in danger, and he had to do everything in his power to stop them.

Moving to the wardrobe, Valermos donned his ceremonial armour. Its golden scales shone against his red skin. Though never intended for use in battle, it was the best he could muster at such short notice. His people had long since moved away from the ways of war, their war with the Terrovore millennia ago had seen to that. What made his people great had long since been lost to the ages, only legend remained.

On the wall sat an ancient blade of red metal, a relic from the times of empire. He removed the sword and clipped it to his belt. The sword, coupled with the pistol he carried for self defence gave Valermos the comfort of being able to take out at least some Voltron before his inevitable demise.

Without further delay, he left his chambers, fearful of the dangers he would encounter outside.

The halls of the palace were surprisingly quiet, despite the explosions and gunfire outside. Valermos swiftly made his way through the long corridors of tapestries until he found himself in the main hall.

The hall was filled with Jovian soldiers, preparing for an attack that could happen at any moment. A man stepped out from them, a human, by all accounts. His name was Tom, the head of his father's personal guard.

'Prince Valermos,' he said as he bowed.

Tom had been posted to Jupiter at the behest of the Earth Alliance. Initially intended for greater things, Tom had requested the transfer to Jupiter himself, leaving behind a promising career in the Alliance Military. Valermos had never gotten to the bottom of that story, but despite knowing little of his past, the two of them had become good friends.

'Where is Sheba? Your father has instructed me to-'

Tom was broken off when a projectile burst its way through the main hall, trampling a selection of the guards and showering them in rubble.

'Where is my father?' Valermos shouted, his ears still ringing from the explosion. His father would know what to do.

'He and his advisors are locked in an emergency session. He asked me to get you away from Jupiter as quickly as possible while he works on a way to bring an end to the conflict.'

'What about the Alliance?' he asked, at a loss to why his people's allies appeared absent from their present predicament. 'Shouldn't they be helping us?'

'Admiral Moore has a fleet on the way as we speak. Until then, we're on our own.'

'I'm not leaving my father.'

'There's no time, Valermos, we have to leave now!'

Another attack landed a bit too close to home. The ground shook and another section of the main hall came tumbling to the ground.

Reluctantly, Valermos had to agree with Tom, and together they left the palace for the city beyond.

The once idyllic City of Jupiter was now a crumbling mess of broken architecture. The Voltron continued their bombardment from the skies, raining death over terrified Jovians with nowhere to flee. Some of them headed indoors, only for the roof to crash down on them as an aircraft passed overhead.

Valermos didn't know where to look, and, more importantly, didn't know what to do. Fortunately for him, Tom did know what to do, and pulled him through the city. They passed several buildings, blazing with fire, the screams of innocent Jovians within. Valermos' heart ached for them, but deep down he knew that there was nothing he could do for them.

The city square was built around the statue of Uberon the Great, who led the Jovian people in their ancient struggle against the Terrovore. Once any visitor would be welcomed by the magnificent sight, now they would be greeted by the countless number of corpses that littered its base.

The bombing ceased, and Valermos caught sight of a jagged Voltron craft land outside the gates of the city, just outside of the square.

'We need to leave the city,' said Tom. 'The Alliance has an agent in place to pick us up once we are away from the fighting.'

'But the Voltron are outside the city!' Valermos felt the sense of being a mouse, about to be caught in a trap.

'It's a risk we'll just have to take. Come on!'

Tom grabbed him by the arm, taking him towards the city gates. There Valermos heard a loud clap, and in seconds he felt the ground escape from beneath him. He flew through the air, hitting the floor with a crack, winding him.

He arched his neck up; Tom was nowhere to be seen. Furthermore, he saw that the city's golden gates had now been blown wide open. Shadows moved just outside his vision. Valermos knew he had to get to his feet.

He scrambled for support, his hands slipped on rocks that littered the floor around him. Something stepped in front of him, and Valermos' instincts told him that he had to defend himself.

The figure before him was a creature born of nightmares. Solid steel armour protected a complex network of wires and circuits, designed to be nimble and adaptable to any environment. Its face, if you could call it a face, was a horrific grimace, painted on a canvas of white metal. The theory behind the grimace was that it would strike fear into the hearts of its enemies, a hypothesis that Valermos himself could confirm.

Staring at him was the face of a Voltron.

Fear seized his body, and he fumbled for his weapon, all the time aware that the creature was reaching out for him with its clawed hand. His fingers felt the grip of his pistol, and he grasped it tightly, bringing it to bear on his enemy. He squeezed the trigger, his eyes closed, terrified of what would happen next. When he opened them, he saw a score mark of the wall behind where the Voltron stood, still smoking. He sighed, turning his head to one side, where once again he caught the gaze of his foe.

He screamed as he expected the Voltron to snuff his life out at any moment, and tried to scrabble away to freedom. His hearts raced until he realised that the robot was motionless, a plume of smoke billowing from its side.

Before he knew it, Valermos was joined by a group of Jovian soldiers. They fussed over him, helping their monarch back to his feet.

'Are you alright, my lord?' one of the soldiers asked him.

'I'm fine,' Valermos replied, though not at all truthfully. 'How are the defences?'

'We're locked in battle across the city. Some of the generals are trying to activate some of the old defences, but so far we haven't seen anything of their success.'

Valermos zoned out as the soldier spoke, his mind taken by concern for Tom, who he hadn't seen since his encounter with the Voltron. 'Have you seen Tom Sanders?' he asked, stopping the soldier mid-sentence.

'Valermos!' called Tom before the soldier had time to speak. Valermos'
heart rang out with joy for the first time since he woke.

Tom had several scrapes down the side of his face, suggesting that he
too had been in some form of engagement since their separation.

'Are you alright?' he asked, showing more concern for Valermos than
his own injuries.

'I'm not too bad,' he admitted, 'considering I've just had my first
encounter with a Voltron.'

'Hopefully it's your last,' added one of the soldiers, moments before
the blast from a Voltron rifle blew him off his feet.

Valermos barely had time to contemplate the irony before Tom had
once again grabbed him by the arm.

With the gates now wide open, they made their escape, cutting down
the invaders as they went. Tom used his rifle to mow down any
Voltron in his path, expertly dispatching them with a single shot each.

Valermos, on the other hand, was more ham-fisted with his pistol
skills, letting off several shots before a single Voltron had been aptly
taken care of.

Outside the gates of the city lay a harsh desert, designed to mimic the
ancient Jovian landscape before its cataclysmic change at the
conclusion of their war with the Terrovore.

The desert, like the city and the palace within, all resided within the
Jovian Atmos-Sphere: a colossal feat of technological engineering that
allowed the Jovian race to remain on their home planet, safely
protected from the harsh environment of modern Jupiter.

Valermos wondered how long the Atmos-Sphere would be able to last
against the current onslaught, as even more ships descended from its
skies.

In the desert, Valermos and Tom found they were able to escape the
epicentre of the battle, though to their dismay, a small Voltron force
were still on their tail.

'I'm out,' announced Tom, throwing his rifle aside as though it were a
children's toy.

'Where is the Alliance agent?' asked Valermos, feeling his lungs burning with exertion in the heat.

'I sent out the signal the moment we left the city. He should be here any minute.'

'He needs to be,' said Valermos, short of breath. 'I don't think I can run any longer.'

'Just a little longer, my prince,' Tom pleaded, looking back to see the Voltron gaining on them.

Valermos lasted another two minutes before he decided he really couldn't go on. His lungs burned and his body was weak. He looked at Tom, who looked to have barely broken a sweat since leaving the city. Valermos concluded that if they did make it off Jupiter alive, that he really needed to get some exercise.

The pursuers were close now, and were almost within range to begin firing.

'Pass me your pistol,' said Tom.

'Why?'

'I'm a better shot.'

'So what will I do?'

'Hope you don't get hit before you can swing that sword at them,' Tom smiled.

Valermos laughed, passing him the pistol. 'For Jupiter?' he said, gripping the sword tightly with both hands.

Tom nodded, and together they stood in wait for the Voltron to come for them.

The ground rumbled.

The Voltron lifted their rifles and took aim.

Valermos gulped.

Tom growled.

The roar of engines burst overhead.

A large blue craft soared across the sky above them, glinting in the sunlight. Large rounds pummelled the ground where the Voltron stood, leaving nothing in its wake but sand.

The ship made another pass, and slowed its approach as it descended towards the desperate duo. A ramp extended from the ship, and a blue-skinned male in Alliance combat gear stood waiting for them. 'Does anyone need a lift?'

Chapter 2

The agent helped Tom and Valermos onto his craft. The doors closed behind them the moment they were on board.

'The name's Black,' the agent said with a wide smile. 'Welcome aboard the *Roc's Feather*.'

The decor of the ship was of a design Valermos had never seen; strange alien text adorned its walls. Almost immediately Valermos could tell that the ship was far in advance of any standard Alliance vessel.

'This ship isn't Alliance issue,' said Tom, echoing his thoughts.

'It belonged to my people,' replied Black, his tone becoming more serious. 'The last of its kind, just like me.' His voice trailed off, his thoughts taken away to a difficult past.

Both Valermos and Tom got the feeling that he was done talking, even more so when he sped away further into the ship. They were left with no choice but to follow. As they passed through the ship's corridors, Valermos could hear the sound of gunfire drumming on the ship's reinforced bulkhead.

The Voltron had found them once again.

They reached the bridge, one of the finest sights that either of the newcomers had ever seen. Computer banks hooked up to a weapons station gave it the feel of a war room, while a row of computers at the front dealt with navigation. In the centre of the room was the captain's chair, which presumably was meant for Black.

Black wasted no time, and set to operate the controls of the bridge with expertise, so much so that he was able to make the ship function as though it had a fully manned crew.

'Do you need a hand?' asked Tom, making Valermos feel guilty for not having offered first.

'It's fine,' he replied. 'Take a seat somewhere. I work better on my own.'

A heavy blast struck one side of the ship, tipping it on its axis. Black was forced to hug the weapons console to balance himself, causing him to admit defeat.

'You,' he pointed at Tom. 'Fly us out of here.'

Tom dashed to the helm and began to operate the alien controls as though it was second nature to him. Black then looked to Valermos, who wore a blank expression on his face.

'Red guy, have you ever been on a Tsani warship before?'

Valermos suddenly got the feeling of a child who had been caught talking in class. Jovian culture had kept its people firmly rooted to their home world, yet another consequence of his people's fear to expand back into space after their war with the Terrovore. As a result of this, Valermos had only read about the craft of other species through the Earth Alliance's extensive archives, a fact that he felt that Black had quickly caught on to.

Without another word, he took Valermos to the weapon console; a network of illuminated buttons and menacing switches.

'Pull this switch here,' said Black, guiding his hands over the console. 'When the lights over here shine red, all you need to do is press that button there.' He pointed to another button on the console, which Valermos pressed when he was told.

It didn't take him long to get used to what Black had taught him. It roughly paralleled the defensive tracking systems of a Venusian Bear-glider, yet another ship he had read about in the Alliance archives. Unlike the Bear-glider, however, Valermos imagined that the systems here on the *Roc's Feather* were far more advanced.

Before long, Valermos had developed quite the talent, racking up a number of hits on the pursuing Voltron vessels.

'The Alliance is here,' announced Black.

He pointed past Tom to the viewscreen, which showed a large number of pencil-shaped ships push their way into orbit above Jupiter.

Tom took the opportunity to bring the *Roc's Feather* out of the Atmos-Sphere, and headed towards the fleet through the harsh weather patterns of Jupiter's natural atmosphere. The ship was buffeted by the harsh winds, but managed to remain on course. The pursuing Voltron ships didn't share their luck, and quickly became lost in the storm. The *Roc's Feather* finally broke orbit, and the three crew members finally saw the full scale of the battle that was being fought around them.

The Voltron fleet numbered in the thousands; a hive of bees scrambling for space around their hive. The ship at the centre of the fleet was towers above the others. Black recognised it menacing design instantly.

'Izak's ship,' he said, spitting out the words as though they were poison.

Valermos had heard the name before: Izak, the mastermind who created the Voltron on a world far beyond the boundaries of Alliance space. Sightings of Izak were rare, as far as the war was concerned. It was far more common to see the Voltron controlled by organic generals, warped to obey Izak's will throughout the galaxy. Valermos assumed that for Izak to be here, a major event of the war had to be unfolding around them.

'Captain Black calling Admiral Moore,' the blue-skinned captain said into the arm of his chair. 'I have a visual on Izak's vessel, moving in to intercept.'

A gruff voice rang out across the channel to meet Black's announcement. 'That's a negative, Captain, your orders are clear: deliver your passengers to Earth. Leave Izak to us.'

Valermos breathed a sigh of relief. As much as he would like for the War to be brought to a premature conclusion, he felt that pitting his newly discovered shooting skills against an entire fleet was not the way to go about it.

'Roger that, Admiral, joining with the fleet now,' he replied through ground teeth.

Tom wasted no time in obeying the order, and took the *Roc's Feather* out of fighting. He nestled it alongside two of the larger Alliance ships, ones designed primarily for troop transport and deployment.

The ship shook once again, and for a brief moment Valermos feared that their safety had been short-lived. He found, however, that the truth was far worse.

Valermos felt a nudge of pain on the tip of his brain, which in moments erupted into a full scale mental trauma. Thousands of voices cried out at once, begging him for help. He clutched his head screaming, as the noise rippled across his mind in waves. His pain was made worse when he recognised some of the voices that called to him, and sensed instantly that something devastating was about to take effect.

The viewscreen switched to a shot of Jupiter. Where moments before, the Atmos-Sphere had floated gently within the planet's giant Red Spot, it now erupted in flame. The fire took on a molten hue, which spread across the Sphere, incinerating buildings and extinguishing the lives within. With nowhere else to go, the fire broke out of the Sphere, causing it to crack like glass. The flames burst outwards, mixing with the cocktail of gases in the outer atmosphere. The resulting combustion obliterated the nearby area, tearing apart even the Voltron ships that lay too close to the destruction. The planet distorted, losing form, and in that moment, the civilisation of Jupiter was gone.

Valermos watched as all traces of his home flickered from existence. The only clue was that same Red Spot, which now took on the heavy colour of blood.

The Jovian retched; the only reaction his body felt appropriate for the travesty he had witnessed. Everything he had once called home had just gone up in smoke. What made it even worse was that he had been utterly powerless, completely unable to stop it. Both Black and Tom looked at him, unable to form any words of comfort. Finally, Valermos fell to his knees, not knowing what else he could do as the pain swirled around him in a fierce cloud of anguish.

Black cursed, as his attention was drawn back to the viewscreen. Deciding that their work was finished, Izak and the Voltron fleet retreated, leaving the Alliance fleet alone above the ravaged remains of Jupiter.

'All ships disengage and return to the Earth for debriefing,' ordered the Admiral, sounding relieved for the battle to be over.

'You heard the man,' said Black, his eyes sullen. Tom took one last pitied look at his friend before plotting the ship on its course.

With tearful eyes, Valermos watched as he was swept from his home. His former world was quickly reduced to just a speck in the distance, a mere pinprick in a sea of infinite night.

Chapter 3

In the depths of space, the Voltron fleet travelled back to its territory, largely unharmed by the attack on Jupiter. On the bridge of the fleet's capital ship, Rern made his way past a number of Voltron guards, his head hung low at all times. He had been sent there with a report, one which he was terrified to deliver in person.

Life as a slave was the worst kind of torment a person could undergo. That torment was made even worse once the Voltron took over. When their fleet first arrived over his home world, he thought that salvation had come at last. It was only after the robots began butchering his people by their millions that he realised things were only going to get worse.

He had only served aboard the ship for a week, but to him it already felt like a lifetime. The Voltron were cruel masters, they had no concept of compassion, or any understanding of organic life. They expected nonstop work from their slaves, and left little time for sleep or nourishment. As Rern approached the bridge's command chair, he couldn't tell whether his hands were shaking from starvation or through pure fear.

Seated on the chair was the Voltron's harrowing leader: Izak. From his perspective, the Voltron leader was largely covered in shadow, yet Rern could see that parts of his body had been entirely replaced by technology. The sight of machinery welded to the flesh left Rern quaking with fear. Despite the trembling in his hands, he began to speak, avoiding eye contact at all times.

'Lord Izak, I have the report from the Battle of Jupiter. Our forces have successfully neutralised the Atmos-Sphere, destabilising their protective environment-'

'I have no time for your overview, I was there,' he snapped. 'You are here to tell me what I need to know. Did we get what we came for?'

Rern continued to shake, vastly intimidated by Izak's menacing tone. He let out a small whimper before speaking further.

'We lost our ground troops when the Atmos-Sphere was destroyed. As a result, our forces failed to recover any Jovian subjects from the planet.'

Izak roared in rage, lifting Rern up by his scalp. The stout alien screamed in terror, believing these moments to be his last. The pressure on his cranium was unbearable, and he begged for the pain to stop. Finally, the Voltron leader relented, dropping him to the floor with a crash. Rern picked himself up quickly, wiping the tears from his eyes.

'My plans would have succeeded if we had not been interrupted by the Alliance fleet. They were pre-warned of our arrival.'

'There have been no leaks reported since the attack on Grace,' Rern explained, reading from the report as quickly as possible. 'If the Earth Alliance were tipped off to our arrival, it must have been-'

'It was the *Roc's Feather*,' Izak interrupted with the upmost certainty. 'Captain Black continues to disrupt my efforts at every turn.'

'The *Roc's Feather* was present during the Battle, Master. We intercepted some chatter from Alliance frequencies; it is possible a Jovian has survived the battle.'

'What is the identity of the survivor?'

'The survivor is believed to be Prince Valermos of Jupiter. Our forces reported his escape from the Jovian city shortly before the planet was destroyed.'

'Where is he now?' Izak leant forward on his chair, a robotic red eye peering down at him. Rern squirmed under the eye's ferocious glow.

'Our intelligence puts him on the *Roc's Feather* at the time of Jupiter's destruction.'

Izak roared again. He lashed out with one hand, slicing through the slave's neck with his razor-like fingertips. Separated from its body, the head fell to the floor. A trail of blood followed it as it rolled towards the door.

His anger unabated, Izak turned to one of the Voltron at his side. 'Contact our agent on Earth. If the Jovian lives, I still have a chance to carry out my plans...'

Chapter 4

The intense feeling of loss swirled through Valermos' head like a hurricane, sweeping away every positive emotion in its wake. As he walked through the streets, he realised that his emotions were detracting from his first experience of an alien world, a dream he had held since he was a boy.

The *Roc's Feather* had taken them to Earth, the city of San Francisco – the very heart of the Earth Alliance. The city was a hub for universal culture, a multitude of species had made a home here since the days before the War broke out.

A Venusian pushed past him, almost dropping the papers it was carrying. It muttered a few words of apology before carrying on, heading for an Alliance Security Force outpost, only to find its hunched frame stuck in the door due to its enormous size. Valermos saw a variety of other species too: a Menith businessman, carrying a briefcase in one of its many arms; Tauran traders, sniffing out bargains with their large snouts; and a Brovian preacher, pointing out to all the folly of their ways. At one point he even thought he saw a Draxi, swept up in the feet of taller beings.

Before long Valermos found that the streets began to close in on him, and not just due to the overpopulation. People began to stare, talking amongst themselves in a variety of languages that he didn't recognise. The Brovian preacher caught sight of Valermos, and interrupted his teachings to proclaim the miracle of his survival. The Brovian's booming voice gathered yet more onlookers, flocking to get a look at this modern day miracle. It seemed that Brovian had also caught Black's attention, which made him yell angrily at those who got in their way.

'Ignore them,' he said, pausing to push a dopy-looking Tetrip out of his way. 'They've obviously heard the news. It looks like you're a celebrity now, my friend.'

'And all I had to do was see the extinction of my people, who'd have thought it?' said Valermos, sarcastically, a pinch of anger in his voice.

'Can you believe I grew up here?' Tom said, casting despairing glances over the people that they passed. He had been in a mood since they had landed, and Valermos was now starting to see why.

'Bad childhood?'

'I'd rather not talk about it,' he replied, visibly closing up. 'Let's just say I was glad to get away.'

'Will both of you just cheer up?' Black shouted after pushing yet more people out of their way. He grinned, trying to bring some happiness out of them. 'We're about to meet the leaders of the Earth Alliance. At least act like you want to meet them!'

In front of them stood The Hourglass, the power seat of the Earth Alliance Council. Four pillars formed the building's exterior, supporting the hourglass structure within. The building was a wonder to behold, and acted as a physical embodiment of the power the Alliance held. The three of them walked up the marble steps to the entrance of the building, where they were greeted by an elderly man in an Alliance uniform. The epaulettes on the uniform showed the man to be an admiral, one of the highest ranks attainable in the Alliance Military. From the look of the man Valermos knew he had seen battle: around his eye he sported a long scar that ran down his cheek, giving him the distinction of a seasoned warrior. Despite this hardened exterior, the man smiled down to them, warm and welcoming.

'Admiral Moore,' said Black, saluting.

Valermos looked to Tom, and saw that he too was saluting, a clear sign of his origins in the military. Not wanting to feel out of place, Valermos also saluted, much to the amusement of the Admiral.

'That's the first time I've had royalty saluting me,' Moore said with a smile. 'We're glad to have you here on Earth, Prince Valermos. On behalf of the Alliance I'd like to extend my condolences to you on the loss of your people. The Jovians were a noble race, and will truly be missed.'

'Thank you, Admiral,' was all that Valermos could manage without his feelings getting the better of him. Moore saw his pain and delicately stepped around the issue.

'Captain Black, your mission was a resounding success. The Council has called an emergency session to discuss the outcome of the Battle of Jupiter, and the steps we must take from here. We better not keep the Council waiting.'

Moore turned and led the trio into the grand halls of The Hourglass. The rooms inside were dedicated to the success of the Alliance throughout history. One room they walked through depicted Humanity's first contact with the Venusians; another showed Nick Cross stood on the rocky shores of Proxima Two, Earth's first colony. As Valermos walked past a statue of Harry Whistle, he wondered if one day there would be a room for the people caught up in the present conflict.

The doors to the Council chambers were guarded by two soldiers in dress uniform. They saluted Moore as he approached, and opened the doors for him without question. Inside the Council waited, each of them stood on platforms that raised them high above their audience. At the back of the circular room was a larger platform, on which stood Umbaste, the President of the Earth Alliance. Dressed in golden robes, the dark-skinned human looked every part the leader. He smiled at Valermos as he entered the room.

'Welcome guests of the Alliance. We are gathered here today to discuss the aftermath of the Battle of Jupiter, a dark day for our Alliance. We will open with a speech from Prince Valermos, sovereign of Jupiter, and sole Jovian survivor.

Valermos' stomach lurched; he had never made a speech before, and had certainly not planned anything to say to an audience. After a moment's thought, he decided that he would speak from the heart, taking inspiration from a lesson his father had taught him at a very young age.

'Earlier today I watched my people die,' he began. *Nothing like an opening line to draw people in,* he thought to himself. 'I saw the Voltron invade my sacred home and destroy everything I hold dear. I am not an angry man by nature, and I am certainly not a warrior, but today I have learnt that the Voltron need to be stopped, whatever the cost. No one else should have to feel the pain that I'm feeling right now, and if we work together we can make sure that the events of today don't repeat themselves.'

A hand was placed on his back. Turning, Valermos saw that the hand belonged to Black. He then remembered that Black too had lost his people to the Voltron. He knew in that moment that both of them were much more alike than either of them had realised.

'Thank you, Prince Valermos,' said Umbaste, showing little empathy with his words. 'The Battle of Jupiter has indeed shown us that the Voltron War has reached a much more alarming level than we had realised. Our enemy have attacked us within our home system. We must now postulate that Earth may well be their next target. The Alliance must stand prepared.'

There was a murmur of agreement across the room.

'Our fleets in the outer systems can be pulled back in defence of the core. Earth has to be our priority,' said Venusian councillor Trask.

'Our most recent intelligence shows that the Draxi have begun to move their ships inwards. I believe we should follow suit and consolidate our forces within this system. Protection of our powerbase is paramount,' agreed Tetrip councillor Sr'pl.

'We can't just retreat!' shouted Valermos, his interruption shocking most of the Council. 'What about the outer colonies, will you really leave all those people for at the Voltron's mercy? I can tell you from experience that the Voltron don't have a compassion circuit.'

'Any civilians wishing to return with the fleet to Earth may do so,' snapped Umbaste. 'We are fighting a war here, Prince Valermos. Sometimes hard decisions must be made.'

'Even when those decisions come at the cost of losing our own humanity?' Tom shouted, quick to leap to his friend's defence, outraged at the selfishness he was witnessing.

Umbaste began to twitch, not used to opposition. 'The decisions that the Council make are for the betterment of the Alliance as a whole, Commander Sanders.'

'The betterment of yourselves, you mean,' added Valermos, fixing the President with an angry stare.

Umbaste straightened himself, trying to bring his twitch back under control. His anger had reached a new level now, and Valermos knew that he had crossed a line.

'I will ignore that comment, Prince Valermos, on the account of your loss. I had hoped that you would one day join this Council and serve beside us. I regret to inform you that will not be the case.'

The door to the chamber opened and the two guards stepped inside. 'The guests of the Council will now wait outside until the session is over.'

The guards approached to escort them out of the chamber. Valermos wasted no time in marching from the room in a fit of rage.

As the doors began to close, both Tom and Valermos saw that Black had chosen to remain behind, and had stepped up to address the Council on his own. Valermos was unable to hear Black's words as the doors shut behind him, and both he and Tom were escorted away to a private atrium at the apex of The Hourglass.

Black stood alone in the centre of the chamber, looking up at the President and the councillors with hope in his eyes. To one side stood Moore, who looked on, unsure if Black was the bravest man he had ever known, or the most foolish.

'Can we help you, Captain?' asked Umbaste, irritated by yet more resistance to the proceedings.

'I appreciate the importance of your time, Lord President, but I feel I must once again ask you to reconsider my proposal.'

Black stood with open arms, hoping to his gods that Valermos had not closed off all the doors to his sense of reason.

'You mean your suicide mission?' said Umbaste, amused.

'I try not to think of it that way,' said Black, his voice confident, and head held high. 'Today we have seen the Voltron strike further into Alliance territory than ever before. I do agree that Earth must be better defended so that it may avoid the same fate as Jupiter, or even my own world, yet while we look to defend, we lose our opportunity to eliminate the source of our distress.'

'You wish to take the fight to Izak?' asked Moore. 'That *is* suicide!'

'Lord President, I have worked for the Alliance for several years now, and my track record surely proves that I can pull this off.'

Umbaste laughed. 'I do not doubt your track record, Captain; your work for the Alliance has not gone unnoticed. I do doubt, however, that even someone with an unblemished record of such as yourself will be able to pull off such a mission alone.'

'That's why I don't plan to do this alone.'

'You have a team in mind?'

Black smiled.

'Lord President, you just met them.'

From the atrium Valermos and Tom could see the entire city stretched out before them. Though Tom himself wasn't in the best of moods, he could see that Valermos was faring much worse.

'You okay?' he asked, barely audible above the sound of Valermos' angry breaths.

'It's all just a talk show to them, isn't it? A whole race of people died today, yet all they cared about was how best to protect themselves.'

'That's politicians for you,' said Tom. 'Why do you think I left home?'

Valermos laughed, despite himself. Tom always did know just the right thing to say.

'You left home because of the politics?'

Tom coughed, feeling uncomfortable. He wasn't used to opening up about his past; there were too many bad memories for him.

'I left because I lost the part of me that was real,' said Tom, deciding that Valermos needed the distraction, even if it was with his own boring back story.

'I spent so much time with the Alliance Military that I wasn't there for the people I loved when they needed me. I lost someone very close to me, and my commanding officers didn't even care. That day I saw that the Alliance didn't care for the little people, and that's just something I couldn't bear to be a part of anymore.'

'Thanks for sticking up for me in there,' said Valermos.

'I stuck up for you because you were right, Valermos: people need protecting and it's the Alliance's duty to do that. If they don't then the Voltron have pretty much won this fight already.'

'Then let's hope that Black was able to change their mind.'

The hours passed and the sun set across San Francisco, bathing the city in moonlight. Tom and Valermos spent their time reminiscing of their time on Jupiter. When they had finally decided to retire for the evening, they were reunited with Black, who was accompanied by Admiral Moore.

'You're back!' said Valermos, filled with excitement. 'What did the Council say to you?'

'They've given me my next mission,' he said, sounding somewhat reserved. 'I'm to take the *Roc's Feather* on a mission to find Izak's whereabouts. Once I've located him, I'm to determine the best measure to take him out.' He looked at them hopefully. 'All I need now is a team to come with me.'

'You can count me in,' said Valermos, needing no persuading. 'Izak destroyed my home; I'll do anything to return the favour.'

'This mission will be dangerous, Valermos, and have no experience of combat,' said Moore, pleading with him to reconsider.

'Then he will need someone to teach him,' said Tom, stepping forwards.

Moore sighed, knowing that no matter what he said, he would never change their minds.

'Then it's decided,' said Black. 'Get some rest, we leave first thing in the morning.'

With a bright look on his face, Valermos departed, closely followed by Tom. Before Black had chance to join them, Moore stepped in, taking him to one side.

'You are aware that you'll be leading them to their deaths,' Moore said to him. His voice sounded more serious than Black had ever heard it before.

'The Alliance is failing, Admiral, just must see it. You've seen Valermos, he's desperate for revenge. These people have nothing to lose; they'll get the job done.'

'So you're saying they're just like you?'

Black took a step back, not knowing whether or not to be insulted. 'I've done many things since I lost my home, Admiral, and not all of them I've been proud of. If we succeed then we will stop any more blood from being spilled. That sounds like a pretty good outcome for the death of three nobodies.'

'Even when the odds are against you, there's always hope, Black, you know that better than most. You just promise me that if there's any chance of you coming home that you'll take it.'

Black held the Admiral's gaze, unsure if he could make that promise. 'What will be, will be, Admiral.'

Far across the rooftops, a shadow watched them. The shadow had a slim, feminine figure; her hair reached far down her back, curved and pointed at its tip like a knife. The shadow's name was Katelyn, and her work was finished.

She turned off her equipment, folding it down to a compact size. She pushed the device into a small backpack and was away. She leapt over rooftops as though they were puddles, scaling half the city in a matter of minutes. Reaching her destination, she scuttled down a drainpipe to street level. From there she had a small walk to a nearby warehouse, which appeared to be abandoned from the outside.

Inside the building it was anything but abandoned: Katelyn had built herself a makeshift home, adorned with all the furnishings and provisions she needed to survive.

By her makeshift bed sat a small computer, which was connected to a large dish by heavy duty cables, designed to amplify the signals it transmitted. She turned on the computer, and typed in the necessary information she needed to open an encrypted call to the stars. She didn't have to wait long for the call to connect. When it did, she was greeted by the grim cyborg face of Izak himself.

'Report,' he barked. Katelyn could feel his glowing red eye upon her, and almost retched as she thought about the way it protruded from his purple flesh.

'It is as you expected, my lord. The Council have appointed Captain Black on a mission to assassinate you.'

Izak sneered. 'I face assassination every day, Katelyn. Give me some intelligence that I can use.'

'Prince Valermos and his bodyguard will be accompanying him on this mission.'

For a moment Katelyn thought she saw a look of fear sweep across his master's face. If the moment did exist, it was gone just as quickly, and the gruesome calm was all that remained.

'The last Jovian,' he said, deep in thought. 'That changes things. I shall dispatch assassins to hunt them down. The Jovian cannot be allowed to interfere in our plans.'

'My lord, shouldn't I be the one to go after them? I'm more than equipped to deal with them.'

'No, you will leave Earth immediately. We have other plans for you.'

The call ended abruptly. Katelyn took one last look at the place she had called home for the past few months. Satisfied, she struck a match and flicked it onto the floor. Within moments everything in sight was ablaze. There was no time for looking back as an agent of the Voltron.

Chapter 5

Valermos couldn't sleep. It was not that his quarters on the *Roc's Feather* were uncomfortable; in fact they quite luxurious. The problem was that when Valermos did try to sleep, he would instantly be plunged into the realm of nightmares. His mind revisited the trauma he had experienced over Jupiter. In one moment he had felt the chatter of a whole civilisation cease with unending silence. His dreams haunted him till the moment he woke, and even then, he wasn't sure that it was a world he wanted to wake to.

Life on the ship was one of hard work, something Valermos had not been used to as Jovian nobility. Tom spent countless hours with him each day, teaching him the arts of combat he had learned during his time at the Academy. So far Valermos had been slow to learn, and his body constantly ached and throbbed with the cuts and bruises Tom had inflicted. It wasn't as if he didn't want to learn, it was the only way they were going to defeat Izak after all; his mind was just on different things. He was aware that some dark, twisted part of his mind welcomed the pain, feeling that he deserved it as punishment for surviving his race's extinction. Valermos tried not to dwell on those thoughts, for he knew that they would never bring them back.

Valermos shook his head, trying to expel the thoughts from his mind. He walked over to the sink and splashed his face with water. He looked in the mirror above the sink, and watched the droplets slide down his crimson face.

Is this the face of a warrior? he wondered, staring into the burnt orange eyes before him. *Perhaps one day*, a voice from the corner of his mind whispered back.

He looked around the room for something to take his mind off things, and was startled by the realisation that his room was so Spartan. The only thing of note was the ancient sword on the wall, the only relic that linked him to his past. Finding nothing to do, Valermos slipped on a pair of boots and headed for the door.

'Perhaps a walk will do me some good,' he said to himself as he stepped into the corridor beyond.

The halls of the *Roc's Feather* were a boring affair; the dim lighting during the evening hours doing nothing to lift his mood. He wondered what the strange script on the walls actually said, and if it would shed any light on the ship's mysterious captain.

During Valermos' brief time on the ship, Black had very much kept to himself, locked away in his quarters or some unknown part of the ship, far away from either himself or Tom. Valermos wondered just what Black was doing with his spare time.

As he continued to wander the corridors, he suddenly remembered one rule Black had made abundantly clear once they had joined the crew of his vessel: no one was to wander the corridors alone unless accompanied by Black himself. After a moment's contemplation, Valermos concluded that if he only spent a few minutes outside his room then Black would be none the wiser.

He decided to spend those few minutes completing a lap of the ship; past the engine room and the sick bay, before doubling back towards his quarters. It was only when he had begun his walk that Valermos realised his route would take him straight past Black's own quarters. Slowing to a shorter pace, he tiptoed past the door. Hearing no sounds from within, Valermos was confident that he had evaded detection, and continued on at his normal pace.

Walking past the sick bay, he felt a strong draft blow against his neck. He traced the draft to the wall opposite its sliding doors, and traced his hands along it. He felt his fingers catch on something, a gap built into the wall. Pushing his index finger into the gap, he was able to slide the wall to one side, revealing a hidden corridor within.

The corridor was coated in dust, save for a select number of footprints, carving out a path for him to follow. The footprints led him to a room bathed in blue light. Inside he found an abundance of medical equipment, of varying origin. A screen displayed a heartbeat monitor, showed a weak pulse clinging to life.

Could this be Black's pulse? wondered Valermos. It would certainly explain why they hadn't seen much of him recently. That didn't add up to him, however, as Black had appeared fit and healthy from their first meeting right through to the last time he saw him.

As he continued to look for clues, he traced the wires from the monitor along the floor to a large white capsule at the back of the room. The glass lid of the capsule was misty with condensation, but he could see something inside through the layer of vapour. He wiped the lid with his sleeve and gasped as the source of the heartbeat was revealed.

There was a man inside the capsule, which he now realised was a survival pod. Like Black, the man had light-blue skin; another of his endangered race. It was clear from through the glass that the man was in bad shape: his skin was much paler than Black's, and his body was unhealthily thin.

'His name is Guard,' said a voice behind him. In the doorway stood Black, silhouetted against the thin blue light.

Valermos felt a pang of fear, a feeling of guilt he hadn't experience since he was a boy, caught leaving the palace after dark.

'I'm sorry, Black, I know I shouldn't be out of my quarters, it's just. . .'

Black ignored Valermos's feeble attempt to explain himself and walked straight past him, stopping beside the pod. He peered down at Guard with sad eyes. In that look Valermos could see instantly the history they had once shared together.

'Who was he?' He asked, hoping he hadn't overstepped the mark.

Black sighed as the memories returned to him, an experience Valermos knew all too well. 'We grew up together on our home world, Tsan. Guard and I were inseparable, even though we came from different Houses. Guard hailed from the House of Guards, where he unsurprisingly got his name. On the day the Voltron invaded, Guard was shot while we made our escape. I carried Guard to this room the moment I fled my world in the *Roc's Feather*. He's been on life support ever since.'

'Can't all this equipment heal him?' Valermos looked to the heaps of alien technology strewn around the room.

'The shot burned out his nervous system. Over the years I've scavenged all the medical technology I could find, but no matter how advanced the equipment, I've never found a way to heal him.'

Valermos thought for a moment, digging through his mountain of memories for something that could help. He looked at his hands, and the answer hit him.

'Jovians have a unique genetic makeup,' he began, giddy with his own cleverness. 'As a species we are capable of remarkable feats of regeneration. If I were to transfuse Guard with some of my blood-'

'Then Guard will begin to recover!' said Black, a flicker of hope glinting in his eyes.

'It's not all that simple,' he explained as he began to rummage through the equipment. 'There's no guarantee my DNA will be a match with your physiology. Adding Tom's DNA to the mix should give us something more to work with.'

Valermos gathered the equipment he needed and headed for the door.

'Valermos,' Black called after him. 'I won't forget this, you know.'

He smiled at the captain and left the room. Black smiled back, and felt something he hadn't in a long time. He patted the side of Guard's life support capsule.

'Until we meet again, my old friend.'

Chapter 6

In the soft light of a dimming star, Katelyn piloted her shuttle towards a small planetoid at the edge of the system. She shuffled in her seat awkwardly; it was clearly made for Voltron use, and the Voltron had no need for comfort. Katelyn often wondered when they would have no need for her.

The readings in the cockpit showed that the planet below was just about habitable, despite the cold temperature. She adjusted the control in her bio-suit to compensate, feeling the thin material already begin to vibrate against her skin as it heated up. She flew the shuttle across a long, tree-covered valley. The leaves on the trees drooped, locked in a constant battle to take in enough light from the sun.

She settled the craft in a small clearing, the heat from the engines exhausting most of the local fauna from much needed moisture. As she climbed out of the cockpit, her feet crunched on the brittle remains of the grass below.

Now that she had arrived at her destination, she brought her wrist device to her mouth to make contact with her superiors. A soft beep from the device informed her that the call had been connected. The interference from local sources made the voice on the other end difficult to hear, but almost at once Katelyn identified it as belonging to General Durova, one of Izak's few organic advisors.

'Report on your status, Agent Katelyn.' Durova's voice was monotone, a clear side-effect of the robotic enhancements forced upon him by Izak.

'I have arrived at the target location, General. The interference on my equipment suggests that the artefact is nearby.'

'The artefact has been marked as top priority. The Voltron Empire must obtain it at all costs. Eliminate anything on this planet you come into contact with. You have been chosen for this mission because of your unique skill set. Do not fail us.'

The call ended abruptly and Katelyn stared up into the harsh rainclouds that loomed overhead. Night was beginning to close in and she was eager to get on with her mission. Everything on this world was caught in an uphill struggle for survival, and she wasn't planning on joining in.

From the moment she set foot on the planet she had become aware of why she had been sent here. Whatever was here on the planet interfered with anything technological. Any Voltron who set foot on the planet would be fried in seconds. Katelyn was here because she was expendable, and she was well aware that one day her usefulness would be at an end. Until that day she would do her duty, earning the money she needed to move on from her current masters.

She moved through the foliage, each footstep slopping in the mud and rain. If there were any hostiles on the planet, a stealth approach was not an option. She drew her pistol, in full preparation for anything she might face.

Moving beyond the valley, her path dropped down into a basin. Vast waterfalls gushed down from all sides. The sound of the water drumming on the ground was deafening. She checked her wrist device, the screen crackled and flickered. She had to be close.

She moved further into the basin, the sound of the waterfalls growing quieter with each step. With the sound fading, she thought she could hear voices past the rocky outcroppings ahead. She crouched down, moving slowly towards the source of the noise. Her pistol was held high, ready to fire at the slightest movement.

Peering over the rock, she spotted a group of small humanoids, clad in simple furs and cloths. They were huddled around a fire, staying close to it for warmth. The creatures were primitive, small spears and sticks were stacked against a nearby tree. She looked upon them with pity. Her foot slipped on the rock, twisting at an unnatural angle. Her gun made a loud crack as she steadied herself. She cursed under her breath and rubbed her ankle, trying to sooth the sharp pains arcing through it.

There was a loud snap, and her heart skipped a beat. In her pain, she had forgotten about the primitives she had been observing. Carefully, she popped her head out from over the rock, closely followed by her weapon. In front of her was one of the primitives, holding its spear out, cautiously. The creature had a confused look on its rodent-like face. She doubted it would have ever set eyes on an alien before, let alone a Human.

From this distance Katelyn could easily dispatch the creature before its spear came close. Yet, instead of striking out in fear, the creature pulled back its spear, and stretched out its hand. Katelyn was confused, expecting some kind of trick. The creature saw no treachery, though, and beckoned Katelyn forwards, inviting her to join its friends at the fire.

Katelyn was taken aback by this request. Her experience of the galaxy was of its many inhabitants shooting at her on sight. She could scarcely count the number of times she had been attacked through fear and ignorance. Right now she was experiencing something completely different: these creatures were showing her compassion. Even though she carried a weapon in her hand, these creatures saw right past it. She didn't know how to react when the creature took her hand and led her over to the fire to meet its brethren. All of the creatures shared a similar appearance; they were coated in short fur, and had teeth that were at sharp as knives. Each of them wore coats made of thicker fur, taken from some other form of creature native to the planet. They all stayed close to the fire, watching as their cold breath evaporated in its proximity.

As she joined the creatures at the fire, she felt her bio-suit adjust to the new temperature. As much as these creatures needed the fire, she didn't need it at all. She was here for another purpose than to keep warm, a task she could delay no longer.

'I'm here to find an artefact,' she told the creatures. They looked back at her with confusion on their faces. Even if she had a translator it was unlikely these creatures would understand her, their minds were too undeveloped for complex language. Soon forgetting about her attempt to communicate with them, they once again returned to the fire, each of them mesmerised by the flickering flames.

Not losing hope, she tried a different approach to commune with them. Tapping the one nearest to her, she showed it her wrist device, the screen still playing up for them to see. Upon seeing the device, the creature leapt up, calling to its friends for them to see. As each of them saw the device, they all shared the same response, leaping up and down in excitement. One of them took her by the hand and led her to the edge of their encampment. There it stopped, pointing at something in the distance.

'What is it?' she asked, as the creature tapped at her wrist and pointed again into the distance. As her eyes slowly adjusted to the gloom, Katelyn could make out a man-made structure built into the cliff face beyond. She thanked the creature - realising that her gesture wasn't likely to be understood - and set out towards the structure.

From even this distance, Katelyn could see that it was a grand construction. If she didn't know better, it seemed to her as though the rock had grown around the structure itself, providing the ultimate concealment. Though most of it was covered in large vines which hung down from the cliff face, the surface of the metal reflected the light from the campfire behind her. This allowed Katelyn to follow the design of the building, leading hopefully to some form of entrance. She made away along a narrow stream, following it along the cliff side until it gave way to a cave mouth, propped open from the rock by two metal girders.

She looked at her wrist device again and saw nothing but static. This had to be the place. Holding her pistol ready she entered the cave, praying that her mission would soon be over.

The cave was pitch black, the darkness embraced Katelyn, not an ounce of light to be seen anywhere. Nevertheless she continued to walk through the cave. She wondered for a moment whether she ought to fire her pistol, using the momentary flash to get a bearing on her surroundings, but thought again as she began to wonder what else might be in the cave with her.

One step, then another, she made her way deeper and deeper onwards. So far as she knew, she had walked in a straight line since she entered. She relied on her other senses to guide her. A gentle breeze blew behind her, which told her she hadn't doubled back on herself. It also gave her the knowledge that if she continued forwards she must soon find something.

Her assumptions proved correct, as the path soon descended, and a small light hummed in the distance. The light was blue, like the skies of Earth. She felt herself drawn to it. It pulled to her, inside her own mind. The light dimmed as she drew near. As her hands touched it, the source of the light leapt into her hand. She looked at the object; a cylindrical device, the size and shape of a flask. When she pulled the object from its housing, every light in the building switched on at once, and Katelyn was bathed in light.

When her eyes adjusted to the light, she found that she was in some sort of chamber, not much different, she realised, to a shrine. The cradle in which the device had been housed looked like a pedestal, and was the only feature of the room. As she moved to leave, she felt something shift in the architecture, and suddenly realised that the entrance of the room was starting to be sealed off.

The Voltron chose their agent well, as Katelyn's agile form had leapt out of the room with moments to spare, and she rolled into the corridor beyond. The door shut behind her with a dull thud. From the moment the door closed, she knew her time was scarce. Within moments she heard the sound of running water, seconds later, the rooms began to fill from the ground up. She moved back through the complex like a cheetah. Since removing the artefact, her wrist device had started working again. She checked the display and found a detailed map of the area, which included her way out.

She followed the map through the now well-lit passageways, the rising water impeding her movement as she travelled. The water had reached her waist, and fatigue was starting to set in.

By the time the water had reached her neck, Katelyn was exhausted. From here she could see the cave mouth, and the dim light of day outside. She willed herself on, her feet kicking at the water as it raised her off the ground.

The water engulfed her. She kicked and kicked with what little strength she had left, but failed to surface.

Slowly her body began to give in. The water forced its way into her nostrils until she gagged, allowing even more water in. She thrashed violently, hopelessly reaching out for salvation. Able to grasp at nothing but water, she finally gave up. She curled into a foetus position and waited for the inevitable to happen.

Cold steel limbs pushed through the water. They held her in a firm grip, and pulled her from the deep. She regained consciousness with a cough, spitting water onto her chest. When her eyes opened, she was met with the cold gaze of a Voltron drone staring back at her.

'Where is the artefact?' it snapped. It gave no thought to her health, all it cared for was its orders.

'It's here,' she gasped, still struggling to steady her breathing. She held out the device and it snatched it from her grasp, passing it to another Voltron stood nearby.

Now she had time to take in her surroundings, she found that the entrance to the cave was now swarming with Voltron. With the technical disturbance lifted from the planet, they had arrived in droves. More were landing with every minute. Large drop ships descended from the skies, consuming the entirety of the world in steel. It was then Katelyn's thoughts turned to the creatures who had shown her to the cave. She burst into a run, past the Voltron and their mission, to the fire where the creatures had huddled together for warmth. All she found there was death. The fire had gone out, and littered around it was the corpses of the primitives, each scored with a single laser burn.

'Your mission was to kill anything in your path.'

She turned to find Durova behind her. The Voltron General stood tall, and was more a hybrid than a man. Wires protruded from his skull, tying a metal jaw to his skull. He was a horror to gaze upon, a prime example of all the Voltron represented.

'These creatures were peaceful,' she spat, feeling the tears form around her eyes.

'The creatures were a threat to our presence here. The information held within those ruins is classified.'

'They were barely able to speak!' She stopped herself, knowing that she had gone too far. Voltron were not ones for arguments. They generally ended with a hole in the chest.

'It seems you need educating on the policies of the Voltron Empire.' He raised a hand, and two Voltron marched over, seizing Katelyn in their grip.

'Take her to Grenik. He will teach her the meaning of obedience.'

Chapter 7

Valermos had been thrashed again. His training was a disaster. No matter which way he tried to handle himself Tom would adapt instantly, delivering yet another beating to his exhausted body. The beatings also served to deliver a killer blow to his confidence. He began to wonder if would last even one encounter with the Voltron. Perhaps he wasn't cut out to be a soldier, after all.

He was so distraught, that when Black had called for them to come to the bridge, it was like music to his ears. While Tom wanted to finish their current session, he wasted no time and almost ran from the room. Arriving on the bridge in record time, they found Black in the captain's chair, carefully studying a set of readouts on the viewscreen. Since Valermos had discovered Guard in the bowels of the ship, Black had become significantly more sociable, even helping with his training when the mood took him. As a consequence life on the *Roc's Feather* had taken a more positive turn. He even felt that Black was beginning to warm to his new crew. Despite this, Valermos couldn't help but feel that there was a whole other side to his captain that they hadn't yet seen; something just under the surface, ready to present itself at any moment.

'What's going on, Black?' asked Tom, heading to his post at navigation.

'We've received a distress signal from a nearby planet,' Black replied. He slumped back in his chair, finished with his assessment of the readouts.

'Is it an Alliance world?' Valermos asked.

'Vamshi,' Tom replied in confirmation. His terminal displayed an image of the planet, complete with basic information about its properties.

'Never heard of it,' Black muttered.

'It's one of the Alliance's furthest outposts,' Tom explained. 'We must be on the very edge of Alliance space.'

'What does the message say?'

'It doesn't say anything,' said Black, 'just a general plea for help, repeating over and over.'

'The worlds at the edge of Alliance space were taken by the Voltron during the opening conflicts of the War,' said Tom. 'There's little to no chance that anyone is still alive down there.'

'The Voltron scorched these worlds years ago,' said Black, his eyes staring out at the rocky planetoid before them. 'I smell a trap.'

Valermos couldn't believe what he was hearing. 'We have a duty to help anyone who could have survived. They're Alliance citizens, Black, we can't just pass by!'

His mind conjured up pictures of Jovians who somehow survived the Voltron attack, left alone in the dark while the Alliance moved on. He wouldn't leave them to their fate, so why should things be any different here?

'We're going down there,' he announced, his voice resonating with a confidence he wasn't aware he possessed.

'Not happening,' Black replied, stopping him in his tracks. 'We're on the boundaries of Voltron space. For all we know Izak could be just a couple of systems away and we can put an end to this war. We can't jeopardise the mission on a fool's errand.'

'Then leave me behind,' said Valermos, refusing to back down. 'We're on this mission to save lives, Black, and that's exactly what I intend to do.'

Black looked to Tom for some support. The whole Alliance was depending on them to complete their mission. Even the slightest delay could cost millions of lives.

'The Vamshi outpost is just a small listening station, Black. It wouldn't take too long for us to check for survivors.'

With no support, Black sighed, defeated. He needed both of them for his mission to stand a chance of succeeding. He cursed, knowing he had to relent.

'In and out,' he said, begrudgingly. 'We look for any survivors and leave, nothing else.'

41

The *Roc's Feather* settled on a docking platform just a short distance from the listening station. The planet's sun was nowhere to be seen; instead the area was lit by small lamps, which shed an artificial green light over the crude path towards the station's entrance.

Valermos' feet crunched on the hard, dead soil, making him wonder how anyone could live out here at all. He looked through the windows of the station, seeing no signs of movement within. He began to wonder if this detour would be a waste of their time, after all.

The doors to the facility opened with a *snap-hiss*, and they were met with a rush of warm air. Inside the foyer, everything was neat and tidy, save for two ornamental plants that had shrivelled through lack of attention.

'You see; I told you this place was deserted,' Black harrumphed, turning to leave.

'Wait,' said Tom, placing the palm of his hand firmly against the wall. 'The heating to these rooms would have switched off long ago if no one was here, yet this place was already warm when we arrived.'

'So it's not as deserted as you thought,' said Valermos, a smug smile on his lips.

Black groaned and reached for his pistol.

'So where's the welcome party?'

With impeccable timing, Black's fears were realised. With a loud click, the doors behind them locked, sealing them in. He leapt to the door in a flash and tried the handle. His hand flicked back with a crackle and a rush of pain.

'A force field,' he said, nursing his injured fingertips.

'We're trapped in here?' Valermos yelped. A horrid sensation formed in his stomach and rose through his body in waves. Fear paralysed him as his mind began to speculate on what awaited them within the eerily quiet rooms beyond.

'"Trapped" is a manner of perspective.' Black cocked his pistol and marched onward. 'The way I see it, something's trapped in here with us.'

Valermos looked to Tom, and saw that he had also drawn his pistol. Tom gestured for him to do the same. Valermos was left with little choice but to swallow his fear, pushing it back down to the pit of his stomach. Drawing the pistol, he prayed to his people's ancient gods that the little training he had received would be enough.

The silence of the place unsettled him. The station still operated as though it was still in use. Everything from the lighting of the rooms to the synchronisation of the lifts operated as normal. It all suggested to him that the crew would show up at any moment to begin their duties, but where were they?

They had been through several rooms now and had seen nothing unexpected. The recreation area was filled with active gym equipment, and video games that were still running. The kitchens were overflowing with mouldy food and grimy surfaces. So far they had no clues as to what was going on at the listening station.

'This is pointless,' said Tom, his impatience hitting a brick wall. 'We need to start looking for some way to switch off the force field.'

'Where do you suggest we start?' asked Black.

'The control room couldn't hurt.'

'Lead the way.'

The control room was a concert of lights. The computers in the room controlled everything, from circulating the air to making sure that every coffee had just the right amount of milk. If there was an answer to their current mystery, they would certainly find it here.

'Where do you suggest we start looking?' Valermos asked.

'We should begin by checking the security footage.'

'Leave it to me,' said Black, striding over to a computer and punching in commands. As he typed, he was blissfully unaware of a disturbing shadow that passed over him.

'It's been wiped.'

'Something's not right here,' Tom said, feeling the hairs on the back of his neck stand on end.

His suspicions were confirmed when a dark mass came crashing down from the ceiling. All of the crew were caught unawares. Black was brought to the floor before either Tom or Valermos could even register what was happening.

It didn't take them long; however, to put things together: standing before them was a six-foot robot coated in thick, black body armour. The robot glared at them through the wide red visor on its helmet-shaped head.

'It's a Voltron assassin,' said Tom.

'A much more robust build of Voltron, complimented with a limited form of artificial intelligence,' added Valermos. 'Yep, I've heard of them.'

The robot assassin stared at each of them, as if contemplating which to attack first. It was only until Tom's agile dive to his left that the robot stepped into action. The robot advanced towards Tom, whose dive positioned him behind a small table. From there he released a series of shots in the assassin's general direction. The blasts that scored a hit only served to slow it down, and delivered very little damage to the robot itself.

Reaching Tom, the robot flipped the table into the air, leaving him completely exposed to its next attack. He winced at the assassin's gargantuan fist came hurtling towards him. Surprise took him when no such blow landed; the robot's attention diverted by several more shots that clanged upon its side like rain on a metal roof.

Behind the robot was Valermos, his pistol smoking from the nozzle. His face was a mixture of fear and surprise. Any surprise from his expression soon faded as the robot turned its back on Tom and marched towards him instead. He released yet more shots on his assailant, each one pinging off its armour like small stones.

The robot reached him, throwing him to the floor with a powerful push. It sped up now, building up the momentum for a killer blow. Something slammed into the side of the assassin, breaking its momentum and momentarily knocking it off balance.

'Not so fast, tin head.'

It was Black. Having regained consciousness, he now had his arms around the robot and was trying hopelessly to use his weight to wrestle it to the floor. The robot swatted him away like a fly, and pressed its attack once more, this time on Black.

Tom rammed a charge pack into his pistol and resumed his attack. As the robot turned away from Black and headed towards him, the spark of an idea ignited inside Valermos' mind.

'Tom,' Valermos said, stressing the urgency with his voice. 'Watch this and see what happens.'

He fired his pistol once, striking the robot on the side of the head. The robot halted its approach towards Tom, turning its attack on Valermos.

'Fire a shot at it, quickly.'

Tom did as he was told. The shot struck the assassin in the back and it halted its assault once more.

'What the hell's it doing?' asked Black, also firing a single shot at their enemy.

'It's like I said,' Valermos began to explain, firing again. 'This Voltron assassin has a limited form of intelligence; very limited, apparently. It's falling for a simple logic conundrum known as Buriden's Ass.'

'Buriden's Ass?' asked Tom, his smile creased with signs of amusement as he fired another shot at the assassin.

'In Earth's early history, a farmer placed a donkey exactly between two bales of hay, the animal starved to death because it couldn't work out which one to go for.' He fired again. 'Why the farmer would want to do that is beyond me, but the concept certainly seems to apply to our metal friend here.'

'I have to say it, kid,' said Black, his voice more earnest than either of them had heard it before. 'I'm impressed.'

After several minutes of constant laser barrage, the robot fell to the ground with a dull thud, without any of its targets harmed. Upon hitting the floor, the assassin's head detached from its body and rolled across the floor, stopping at Valermos' feet. He picked it up and held it aloft in his hand, staring into its lifeless visor.

'What is it?' asked Tom, trying to ascertain what he was thinking.

'This thing had to come from somewhere,' explained Valermos. 'If I can hack into its memory unit, maybe we can find out where it came from.'

'You're not bringing that thing onto my ship,' said Black, sternly.

'Black, I think Valermos is onto something here. This thing had to be sent from somewhere. Assassin droids aren't your bog-standard Voltron variant; records of them are scarce in the Alliance databanks. This thing was sent from somewhere important, specifically to trap us here on this planet. Something's telling me that it was sent by Izak himself.'

Black groaned, looking at the severed robotic head with a large dose of uneasiness. 'Alright, Valermos, you've earned this one. This just better be worth it.' He stepped over to a computer and shut down the command placing the force field over the station. 'Now come on, let's get out of here before something else falls from the ceiling to kill us.'

Chapter 8

From the ship's window, Katelyn looked down at the planet below. This was the world of Das Grenik, Izak's right hand man. It was located somewhere deep in the heart of Voltron territory, the core of the Empire itself. The planet was one of the most fortified worlds in the Empire, second only to the Voltron homeworld itself.

She could see a vast estate; buildings of harsh metal that rose up to the skies in sharp spikes. Voltron patrolled the vast gardens, walking in their hundreds back and forth.

A deep sense of fear built from within. She knew exactly why she was here, and that made the feeling even worse. Her mind harked back to the decimated corpses of the primitive beings. The lack of compassion in the Voltron made her stomach tighten, and she saw, not for the first time, the true atrocity of her employers.

She had been sent to this world to fix all of that. The Voltron knew that it wasn't their beliefs that needed altering; their edict demanded that Katelyn be the one that was fixed. If she was to continue her employment with the Voltron, she first had to be purged of all emotion, whether that was her choice or not.

The ship landed on a tall platform overlooking the venue. Before she even thought about standing, a Voltron hoisted her up to her feet. She stumbled as she felt dizzy with the sudden blood rush. The Voltron showed no concern for her feelings and dragged her from the ship. The outside air hit her in a blast of heat. While the planet was indeed tropical, Katelyn suspected that the source of that heat actually came from the many factories that littered the planet's surface.

A small man was there to greet Katelyn as she exited the ship; at least, something that used to be a man. Tubes burrowed deep into his skin, and a selection of wires and lights pulsed from beneath the surface, giving him an almost translucent appearance. She knew this man immediately to be Das Grenik, the owner of the planet.

'Welcome to Indus, Agent Katelyn.' His voice was coarse, and partially augmented by technology. The sound grated on her nerves, making her shudder.

'What do you want from me, Grenik?'

Grenik slipped a perverse smile. His synthetic lips creased and a blue liquid lay visible beneath the skin. Katelyn could scarcely imagine the extent to which Grenik had augmented himself.

'You know why you are here, Agent Katelyn. Your use to the Voltron as an organic being as reached its conclusion. To continue your services for us, you must first take a step towards the Voltron way of living.'

My fears confirmed, she thought. She knew she had to find some way to escape, yet all routes off the world meant dealing with the Voltron. Clashing with one or two Voltron wouldn't be a problem, not for her skill set, yet when every inch of the planet was crawling with them, she knew escape was simply impossible. As if to confirm this thought, two Voltron closed in on her, clamping her arms in their vice-like grip.

Katelyn was taken deep into Grenik's lair: a dungeon-like complex where monstrous experiments were conducted in the name of science. She caught several glimpses of grim rooms, where invasive operations were being performed. A large variety of species, including Draxi, Tetrips and Humans, all in various stages of surgery, begged and pleaded for mercy. Each of them lay in various stages of receiving some form of cybernetic implantation, all directly interfacing with the subject's brain. Katelyn began to hyperventilate as she realised that she too would soon experience such an operation.

She began to struggle as her thoughts became too much for her to bear. Her dainty arms wrestled against her Voltron escort, but to no avail. The Voltron holding her were too strong, and were able to hold her arms in place with minimum effort. Refusing to give in, she kicked and wailed through the remainder of her trip through the complex. Her screams could be heard by every hopeless soul that still held onto a free thought.

Passing the operation rooms, they entered a much deeper part of the complex. The area was clinical, and appeared to Katelyn not too dissimilar to a hospital. In a large open room, Grenik waited for her beside a large operating table, clothed in surgical attire. Whilst Katelyn already found his appearance unsettling, she was far more disturbed by this change of clothes, as they pushed her anxious thoughts into the realms of reality.

'Welcome to my laboratory, Agent Katelyn. This room has seen the genesis of many Voltron accomplishments. In a few short moments I will begin your augmentation procedure. Rest assured that you are in safe hands.'

'You're a sick man, Grenik,' she spat, her fear quickly turning to anger.

'You speak like an organic, Agent Katelyn,' Grenik laughed. 'I have not been a man in a very long time.'

Katelyn growled, and directed her anger in another way. She swept her foot down on the Voltron to her left. The force of the blow broke her ankle instantly, resulting in a loud crack. The attack loosened the robot's grip on her arm. Fighting back the pain, she reached for its weapon, bringing it around quickly to dispatch the other Voltron holding down her right arm. Now free of her restraints, she levelled the gun at Grenik. The Voltron scientist held her gaze, and showed little sign of fear.

'There is no escape for you, Agent Katelyn. Submit to the Voltron, it is the only option.'

'I will not serve the Voltron anymore.'

She fired the weapon. A thin green bolt zipped from the muzzle, and headed straight for Grenik. Katelyn found herself holding her breath as she waited for her shot to find its mark. The bolt crackled and hissed as it struck Grenik square in the chest. The energy dissipated quickly, and Katelyn found to her dismay that her target was still standing.

'You must think me a fool if you thought I wouldn't come unprepared, Agent Katelyn. You were one of our best agents. Now we shall make you so much more.'

Steel hands came at her from the shadows. She batted them away, desperate to resist, but the hands kept coming. The Voltron were all around her, bleeding from the darkness like demons. She fired her weapon blindly, unable to stop the coming tide. She gave in to it; her weapon clattered to the floor, and the Voltron swarmed all around. Katelyn was dragged, forcibly, towards the operating table. Grenik awaited her, a cruel smile on his lips. As each laboured step passed, she felt herself drawing closer and closer to the end.

Her head was shaved by an unseen hand, and she was hoisted onto the table, kicking and screaming. With a Voltron pinning down each of her limbs, she was strapped onto the table with thick clamps, making escape impossible.

In one movement, the Voltron stepped away. Katelyn was left staring at the ceiling, where a strong light shone down, dazzling her eyes. She blinked as fuzzy patterns spread across her retina. When her vision cleared, she found Grenik towering over her.

'The process is simple, Agent Katelyn. During the procedure, I will be inserting this device into your skull.' He picked up a small microchip and held it between his thumb and forefinger. The device itself looked harmless, yet she knew from Grenik's reputation that his creations were far from harmless.

'The device will interface directly with your subconscious, nullifying your emotions. It will also ensure that you never again deviate from Voltron instruction.'

Grenik placed the device onto his table and switched it for a scalpel. He sharpened the tool for a moment, and paused before he continued.

'Lord Izak has great plans for you, Agent Katelyn. He authorised this procedure so that you wouldn't disappoint him.'

'Izak can go to hell,' spat Katelyn, and she truly meant it. The Voltron had been a means to an end when she had started working for them, a necessary evil. Now she hated them with every fibre of her being. Her wrists struggled against the restraints, and her frustration grew as they refused to budge. Katelyn's temper was building, and she had no way to vent it.

Grenik held the scalpel aloft in his hand, and moved in close to start the first incision. Katelyn roared in anger, and felt tears forming in her eyes as her entire body raged against her situation. She spat in his eye and Grenik flinched, for a moment stopping in his tracks. He wiped it away, and for a moment Katelyn thought she saw a flicker of anger his eyes.

'There is no use in resistance now, Agent Katelyn,' he said, regaining all composure. 'Submit to the process, it will hurt far less.'

Grenik gripped her head in one swift movement. In another he began the procedure, slicing into her cold scalp. Katelyn screamed as she was offered no anaesthetic, and every nerve in her head set alight with pain. Her screams were the last thing she was aware of before her mind gave out from the pain.

Chapter 9

Valermos ran through the desert, she followed behind him. She held his hand tight as they ran across the dunes. They didn't know why they were running or where they were headed. A large rock ahead of them just seemed like the perfect place to be. They ran towards it, not caring about their surroundings, just for each other.

When Valermos reached the rock, he felt her hand slip away from his. Turning to look at her, he found that she was a great distance away. A mountain rose from the ground to block the way. As Valermos tried to scale the mountain, he found himself falling, falling through the very floor itself.

Valermos woke with a jolt. Sweat dripped from his forehead. He wiped it with his sleeve and gasped.

It had all been a dream.

He rose from his bed, walking over to the sink. He splashed his face with water to wake him, and all memory of his dream was forgotten. He looked over to his desk and saw the head of the Voltron assassin staring back at him. Even though it was now lifeless, the blank gaze through its visor still sent a shiver down his spine. After quickly dressing, he picked the head up and left his quarters, headed for the bridge.

Occupying the bridge were Black and Tom, who greeted Valermos with a casual nod as he entered. He moved to his station and planted the head down on the desk. He plugged a wire into the back of the head, and it began to hum and vibrate.

'Have you had any luck with that thing, yet?' asked Black. 'I don't like having that thing on board. Just a few days ago that thing tried to kill us, you know.'

'Nothing as of yet,' admitted Valermos. 'Voltron cybernetics are completely alien to me. I've created a decryption program which should be able to solve the problem. It just needs time to complete.'

'How much time, Valermos? We're living on borrowed time here.'

'The Alliance has no presence out in this area of space, Black,' said Tom. 'The chance of the Voltron finding us out here is minimal.'

'That assassin was able to find us much quicker than I had anticipated. Based on that alone it won't be long before this area of space is crawling with Voltron ships, and all of them will be looking for us. We have to find Izak long before that happens.'

Black had a point, Valermos thought. After only their first stop since leaving Earth, they had encountered a Voltron agent, even if it was due to his own eagerness. Perhaps the Voltron were closer behind them than they initially thought. He checked the status of the decryption: only five percent complete so far. Anxious thoughts grew in his mind and he wondered just how close the Voltron could be at this very moment.

'Tom, could you scan for nearby ships? If there is no chance of us encountering any Alliance ships, then we should have the ship alert us if it picks up anything nearby.'

At navigation, Tom brought up the scanner. The display showed a miniature model of the star system in which they were situated. There were seven planets in the local vicinity, and near the star itself was an abnormal dot.

'What's that?' asked Black, pointing at the dot.

'I'm not sure,' admitted Tom. 'It looks like a ship, and a large one at that.'

'How could a ship get that close to a star?' asked Valermos. 'The shielding alone would require immense power to fuel it.'

'Perhaps it's a space station. There have been rumours going around for years that Izak has one built somewhere. If that's the case, then we could have stumbled upon Izak's whereabouts completely by chance.'

An intense fire burned within Black's eyes. Black's hatred for Izak was like nothing Valermos had ever seen, and he saw how deeply he wanted it to be the case.

'Then we go find out what it is,' Valermos said, and watched Black's face light up.

'I'll bring us in for a closer look.' Tom negotiated the navigation controls for the manoeuvre.

The *Roc's Feather* adjusted its course, heading directly for the sun. The moment it did so, warning lights flashed across the ship, alerting the crew to the fatality that their destination could bring. Black passed his hand over the edge of his chair and silenced the alarm in a nonchalant manner, refusing to remove his eyes from the viewscreen.

The ship shone like a star itself against the harsh light that glared in its direction. Tom noticed the increasing strain on the shields, and directed more power from the engines to compensate.

In the blink of an eye, the light from the star dimmed, noticeably. The light diminished to a mere fraction of its former glow. While trying to discover the source of this anomaly, Tom noticed that the light from his terminal was also beginning to flicker and die.

'What's happening?' asked Valermos, the panic evident in his voice.

'Something's draining the engines,' Tom replied, checking the diagnostics on his terminal before it went black.

'Someone better tell me what is happening to my ship,' said Black, angrily.

'I think it's that ship. It's draining all power in the nearby area, including that sun!'

Black rose from his chair and began to pace the room. The *Roc's Feather* was his prized possession, and more than that, his home. The thought that the ship was powerless was unbearable for him to conceive. He peered out at the mysterious ship with a vengeful look in his eyes. A moment later, he coiled back, as if catching sight of a new revelation.

'That's not a Voltron ship.'

Valermos' ears pricked up, and he went to join Black at the viewscreen. The ship was large, around five miles in diameter. The design of the craft was far in advance of anything either of them had ever seen. They failed to ascertain the function of the large dishes on the ship's aft side, nor the huge cylinders adjoined to its rear. The ship was alien itself.

'If it's not Voltron, then what the hell is it?'

'My first guess would be a Xiz ship,' said Black. 'But even they haven't been able to master stellar technology yet.'

'But the Xiz are the most advanced species in the galaxy!' Valermos exclaimed.

'Then whatever's out there must be even more powerful,' Tom chirped up from behind them.

'Let's get over there, then.' Black gave Valermos a slap on the back and ran across the length of the bridge to the exit.

'And how do you plan to do that? The ship has lost all power.'

'I have some jetpacks in storage that belonged to the original crew,' Black shouted behind him as he left the room. Tom and Valermos shared a look as they both began to speculate the old crew's fate.

Valermos stood on the lip of the exit hanger, and stared out at the vastness of space beyond the edge. Of course he had travelled through space before, but that was always within the safe confines of a star ship. What Black had them planning here was, in Valermos' opinion, nothing short of suicide.

The three of them were clad head-to-toe in Alliance-issue space armour. The highly specialist clothing looked like normal combat gear, which fit tightly to the skin while providing maximum protection in all environments. While the protection was absolute, Valermos still felt uneasy about what they were preparing to do.

'On the count of three,' announced Black. Valermos felt his heart skip a beat.

'Three.'

His stomach lurched, and his thoughts quickly centred on bailing out.
'Two.'
He looked to Tom, who stared ruthlessly at their target.
'One.'
Black pushed his feet off the ground; his jetpack flared beneath him and he was forced upwards. Valermos heard another jetpack ignite and moved his hand over to start his. Upon doing so, he felt his entire body freeze, paralyzed in fear. His head felt woozy and his mouth was dry. Within seconds he had become a bag of nerves, and hated himself for it. He sighed as his thoughts collapsed and he finally gave up. Before he had chance to turn around and head back into the ship, he felt his whole body lift off the floor. Instantly he checked his jetpack, and to his surprise it was still switched off.
'I thought you were skipping out on us,' said Tom, who had picked him up and dragged him on using his own fuel. Valermos could have cried, and his fears melted away instantly. Only pride remained as his old friend had once again picked him up when he was scared. Firing up his own jetpack, he joined the two of them as they soared through space towards the alien vessel.
The exterior of the craft was composed of an unusual alloy. Their weapons had limited effect on breaching it. Running low on oxygen and fearing suffocation in space, their only option was to enter through a small duct near the propulsion systems.

After what felt like hours crawling through the bowels of a complex ventilation system, they finally re-emerged in the middle of a huge banquet hall. A huge table ran the length of the room, surrounded by chairs that were tall enough to seat giants.
'I've never seen anything like it,' said Black. He jumped on one of the chairs, and was astounded when his head couldn't even reach over its back.
'It's like a dollhouse,' said Tom, as he examined cutlery as large as his arm. 'The inhabitants must be huge.'

'Oh dear.'

Black jumped down from the chair and hastily rejoined his companions. He had an alarmed look on his face, and the others quickly saw why: a blue light was starting to surround his body like a mist.

'What is it?' asked Valermos, moving his hand through the light. The light did not budge when he did so, and only proceeded to grow in intensity.

'It's on me, too,' said Tom, who held out his hands to show the others. When Valermos also began to shimmer, they finally started to work out what was happening.

'It looks like a-'

The three of them watched as their surroundings began to fade away. The banquet table melted into a thousand colours, whirling around in infinity. All familiar shapes blurred away, until they were eventually replaced by what looked like a throne room.

'Teleport,' finished Black, smugly.

Tall figures stood all around them, who slowly came into focus, revealing animals with enviable upper body strength. The grey-furred beasts held large spears in their herculean arms, giving them the appearance of a tribal species.

The focal point of the room was a tall throne, on which sat another of the ship's inhabitants. This alien was decorated in a large cloak; his spear was more lavish than the others. This marked him out as the leader.

While initially showing clear signs of nerves, Black quickly regained composure. He straightened his back and stepped forward to address the creatures.

'Hello,' he began, for one of the few times in his life unsure what to say. 'My name is Captain Black. I represent the Earth Alliance vessel the *Roc's Feather*. We intend to come in peace.'

'Your use of primitive language offends me, inhabitant of Galaxy 3521. I am Julnah of the Helicron Empire, and you are trespassing in our territory.' The Helicron leader unfurled its lips, revealing sharp rows of teeth behind. Valermos and Tom took an instinctive step back from the creature. Black instead held his ground, and looked Julnah deep in the eyes and held his gaze.

'We had no intention of trespassing, Julnah,' began Black. 'Our ship was passing by when its power was disabled. We traced the outage here and came aboard to find out what was going on.'

'Your ship's loss of power served our goals,' Julnah sneered. 'The energy from this solar region fuels our war effort.'

'We too are at war. A species called the Voltron inhabits this area of space. They are fixated on wiping out all organic life, which would include the Helicron. Why don't you join with us and use your resources against them?'

To Black's surprise, the entire retinue of Helicron in the room erupted in laughter. They clashed their spears on the ground and roared. Black and the others reached for their weapons, ready for any sudden hostility.

'The Helicron Empire cares little for your puny squabbles. Once our reconnaissance here is over, we will bring the full might of the Helicron armada down on your galaxy. All species in Galaxy 3521 will be destroyed, including your Voltron!' Julnah slammed his spear on the ground and the Helicron roared once more. Tom pulled Black close.

'Black, we need to get out of here now.'

Black's eyes scouted the room, searching for any form of exit, no matter how desperate.

'I'm open to suggestion,' he said finally, admitting defeat.

The Helicron chorus began to subside, and the three of them knew that time was scarce. To their horror, Julnah rose from his throne, and held his spear aloft, preparing to strike.

Valermos decided it was up to him to get them out of this. He had to think on his feet. He looked to his side, and noticed that one of the creatures was in arm's reach. He took Tom's hand and lunged for the gargantuan being, grabbing at its wrist. Tom saw what Valermos was doing and quickly pulled Black close.

Their surroundings began to fade once more. The threat of Julnah's spear dissolved into fuzzy blocks of grey, and the teleport whisked them away to parts unknown.

When their surroundings solidified, Black, Valermos and Tom found themselves in a huge room filled with large cylinders of fluid. The cylinders hummed with energy, so much so that the floor itself vibrated. Before they were able to take in these surroundings; however, the disconcerting shape of a Helicron warrior manifested alongside Valermos.

'Guys!' Valermos squealed, stumbling backwards, ripping the teleport from the Helicron's wrist as he fell.

Tom was the first to react. His military training kicked in and he drew his weapon and aimed in one motion. He pulled the trigger and fired three shots. Each shot found its mark, but the creature only suffered superficial damage to its thick hide.

The Helicron roared in anger. It cursed in its own language and launched itself at Tom. The beast collided with extreme force, and Tom clattered to the floor, fighting for consciousness.

Black joined the fight, aiming for their attacker's head. Two shots were fired, yet only one struck his target. The creature yelped with a loud screech of pain, which almost deafened them. The shots successfully captured the Helicron's attention, and it headed for Black in a bull-like charge.

Valermos picked himself up off the floor as the Helicron began its charge, and all thoughts left his mind. He ran for the creature, intercepting its charge halfway. While some part of his mind expected him to match his enemy's strength and stop it in its tracks, he instead found himself clinging to its back as the charge continued. Refusing to give up, he reached out his hands, feeling for the face. He felt his fingers touch something squelchy, and dug his nails in deep.

The Helicron bucked Valermos from its back, now in more pain than ever. Its roar shook the room, and refused to cease. Black took his chance and aimed at the creature's mouth, unleashing the remainder of his round in quick succession. The shots burrowed into the tender regions of his mouth and burst out through the top of the skull. In seconds the Helicron warrior was silenced, and crashed to the floor in a dull heap.

Valermos ran to Tom immediately, and slapped his face gently to bring him round. His eyes opened in alarm and he squinted as they tried to regain focus.

'Valermos?' Tom asked, recognising his blood-soaked face.

'Yeah, Tom, it's me.' He smiled warmly, and helped him to his feet.

'I'm used to this being the other way around,' Tom laughed as he dusted himself down.

'I've got to hand it to you, kid,' said Black. 'That was quite the thing you did back there. We would both have been goners if you hadn't have stepped in.'

Valermos was so shocked that his jaw almost fell open. Since joining the *Roc's Feather*, Black had scarcely even acknowledged that he and Tom had feelings, let alone paid a compliment. For the first time on their mission, he had not felt useless in a fight.

'There'll be more Helicron on the way,' Tom said, cutting the moment short. 'We need to get off this ship right away.'

'We can't just leave,' said Black. 'This ship is still draining the *Roc's Feather's* engines. We have to destroy it if we're to escape at all.'

Tom examined one of the room's large cylinders, and the seeds of an idea began to the sprout in his mind.

'These look like batteries to me,' he said, his full idea still held close to his chest.

'What are you thinking?' asked Valermos.

'I'm thinking that these cylinders are storing the power that the ship is drawing from the nearby area. If that's the case, then they are basically just huge batteries. Alliance fuel systems usually have some kind of cut off point so that they don't overheat or build up too much power.'

Black caught sight of what they needed, and walked over to a system terminal at the centre of the room. The display was filled with strange alien characters, of which none of them could decipher in the time they had.

'What do we do?' asked Valermos, becoming increasingly aware of how little time they had left before the room was flooded with Helicron.

'Simple.'

Black held out his pistol and pointed it at the terminal, shielding his eyes. With a snap and a hiss, the screen exploded, and klaxons sounded across the ship. Already they could see that the energy levels in the battery cylinders were rising to dangerous levels, and a sense of urgency swiftly became present.

'Come on, let's get going.' Black turned to leave.

'Hold on,' Valermos called after him. 'We'll never make it back to the *Roc's Feather* by the time this place explodes.'

'Then why are you dawdling?' Black cried, irritably. 'Come on!'

'There's no need,' said Valermos, a smug smile on his face. 'Come over here, we can leave using this.'

He held up the Helicron's teleport device in his hand. He fiddled with the settings on the device for a moment, fine-tuning it for their needs.

'How do you know how to use that thing?'

'There were designs for similar devices in the archives back on Jupiter. I studied them for years, but never had the resources to build my own.'

He reached out to his friends and pulled them in close. A moment later the device was activated, and they all began to glow with a fine blue hue.

In the doorway, Julnah and his guards entered the room. They saw instantly the damage that had been done to their ship, and all ran for the intruders. Before any of the Helicron came anywhere close to striking distance, the interlopers had vanished, safely tucked away aboard their own ship.

In the confines of his quarters, Black sat down on his bunk, relieved that their encounter with the Helicron was over. In recent years his thoughts had centred solely on the Voltron, and he had not for a second thought that there were greater threats out there. He lived in hope that with the destruction of this Helicron vessel, the arrival of any more would be prolonged to a date far in the future. For the moment he had the Voltron to contend with, and that was enough.

He walked to his safe and punched in the code without need to see the combination. Inside was a metal container, which he removed and placed delicately on his desk. Black removed a number of small explosive charges from the box and set them neatly alongside each other.

In front of him now were the only tools he needed to exact his revenge on Izak. He sat for a moment, staring at the explosives, looking forward to the day his sacrifice would bring down an empire. He enjoyed this fantasy, and had spent several other occasions just like this, dreaming that the fantasy would one day become a reality.

This time; however, something was different. This time Black looked at the explosives on the desk and felt a sense of nausea. He could scarcely handle the sight of the canisters and their minute detonator, and felt the compulsion to lock them back in the safe and never open it again. His mind searched a long time for the cause of this symptom before the answer came to him with an emotional shockwave that almost brought him to tears.

Black had set out on this mission with companions, expendable additions to his crew that had gained the mission the blessing of the Earth Alliance. At first, he had cared little for them, believing that he could complete the mission alone. Since then, Valermos and Tom had saved his neck on several occasions, and part of him had even started to care for them.

He began to feel frustrated, angry with himself. In the next few weeks he could have the chance to destroy Izak, but would his emotions get in the way of all he ever wanted?

He slammed his fist on the table, and left the room in a fit of rage, knocking his chair on its side as he did so. The chair hit the desk, and caused the detonator to spin around. The spinning continued, refusing to stop until the captain made his choice.

Chapter 10

Through the viewscreen of the *Roc's Feather*, Black could see out into the infinite vastness of space. When he was alone on the bridge, he often stared out at the stars, his mind stretching out in search of his age-old enemy.

He had held this sole quest for vengeance for many years now, more than he cared to recall. His search for Izak had consumed his life; occupying his every waking thought. The memories of his previous life haunted him, the faces he would never again see.

Above all he missed Guard. The trips to his healing chamber had become less frequent since Valermos had discovered it. The Jovian's questions had brought up too many old memories, and the feeling of pain that came with it.

Black longed for closure, he wished for anything to take his pain away. Over on the desk to his left was his chance at that: the head of the Voltron assassin that had hunted them on Vamshi. He had first opposed the notion of bringing the head on board, his hatred of artificial life so great, but conceded after he acknowledged it was a means to an end.

Valermos' encryption program was complete, and the information within the robot's memory had revealed the location of a top secret space station, which was also the last known location of Izak. In the morning the *Roc's Feather* would arrive at the station, and Black's day of retribution would finally be at hand.

When the morning came, Black was ready. He had arrived on the bridge long before Valermos and Tom, and sat waiting for them when they entered the room.

'Battle stations, people.'

Black pushed his hands down on the arms of his chair. He couldn't wait to get things under way, yet knew he had to keep his feelings under wraps.

Valermos passed him, and caught sight of his clenched fists. After quickly flexing them, he was relieved when the Jovian dismissed any questioning thoughts and preceded to his station.

'We're coming up on the coordinates now, Captain,' said Tom.

'Get us within visual range and try to shield us from their short range scanners.'

Tom worked the controls and placed the ship on its course. He brought the ship towards a series of asteroids, which floated innocently at a relatively safe distance from their target. Tom settled the ship atop of one of the asteroids, the ship juddering upon landing.

'I'm still not seeing the station,' commented Black, irritably.

'Wait for it,' Tom replied.

As the asteroid curved and spun its way through space, it gradually brought the enemy space station into view. Tom sat back in his seat and smiled.

The Voltron space station resembled a huge diamond; many sided and virtually indestructible. The walls of the station were mounted with huge cannons, and Voltron ships swarmed its perimeter, both providing constant protection from outside threat.

'It looks impregnable,' Valermos remarked.

'But not invulnerable.'

Black simply could not afford to give up, not now that he had got this far. Despite the seemingly impregnable defences the space station had to have a weakness of some kind, one which he intended to exploit. He looked out of the viewscreen, and saw that a large dispatch of Voltron ships was flying towards the station in a long line, presumably to deliver supplies or refuel. Black realised that this was his chance, and he leapt out of his seat to take it.

'Tom, follow those ships!'

'That's suicide,' said Valermos. 'They'll kill us!'

Tom hesitated to see if Black would change his mind.

'I said FOLLOW THEM!'

Black's outburst made Tom almost leap out of his chair. Without a further word, he followed Black's orders. The *Roc's Feather* rose off the asteroid and headed straight for the Voltron ships.

Black felt the need to reign himself in. His behaviour was uncalled for, and he felt ashamed for taking his inner turmoil on the others. The volatile cocktail of emotions within was threatening to overwhelm him. The majority of his thoughts rested on boarding that space station, while the others debated his actions once he got there. If the mission was to succeed then he knew that the three of them would die making it happen, yet a growing part of him wished that this wasn't the case. Over the last few months he had grown increasingly fond of both Valermos and Tom, and the way he was deceiving them ate him up inside.

Should I tell them?

The thought popped into his head every so often. He imagined their reactions if he did: the two of them would be furious, and not only would he lose their friendship, but the mission would also fall apart if he was to continue alone. Again, Black made the decision to keep his plans private, and focused his mind on continuing the mission.

'Match their speed, try to join their formation.'

Tom did as he was told, not daring to do otherwise. He kept his course steady, and they slowly floated into formation with the enemy ships. To the surprise of all on board, the Voltron ships did not recognise an intruder amongst them, and simply allowed the addition to their number unopposed.

Black smiled in triumph, and dragged himself up from his seat.

'Stay with the ships. When we reach the hanger bay, land us somewhere discreet, away from cameras.'

Black left the room, leaving Tom and Valermos to speculate where he was going.

The corridors of the *Roc's Feather* seemed longer than normal, and each step Black took through them felt heavier than the last. He reached his quarters, and stood quietly in the doorway, unable to move, fighting the inner turmoil with all his might.

On the desk sat the explosives, the tools he had prepared to ensure his plan would succeed. There was just enough firepower in the explosives to obliterate the space station, so long as they were placed in the right areas.

Summoning the strength to enter, he strode over to the desk and swiped all the explosives into a small satchel that hung from his shoulder.

'This one's for you, Guard.'

Black was more than happy with Tom's piloting; he had tucked the *Roc's Feather* at the corner of the space station's main hanger, where it skulked away in the shadows. The crew waited for the inhabitants of the Voltron ships to vacate their vehicles before exiting the ship.

'What's the plan?' Valermos asked, unsure how to go about infiltrating a major Voltron stronghold.

Black felt himself freeze up. This was the moment where he revealed his plan to the others. His first thought was to tell them the truth: that he planned for them all to die in this mission, taking the enemy with them. The words hung on the edge of his tongue, but he found himself unable to send them past his lips.

'Take some of these.' He placed his hand in the satchel and passed three explosives to Tom and three more to Valermos. 'They need to be placed as far apart as possible from each other. This will ensure that their explosive power covers a larger area, taking as much of the station as we can with it.'

They took the explosives from him, examining them closely. Valermos in particular fearfully contemplated the destructive power that he held in his hands.

'How long are the charges set once they're live?' asked Tom, showing clear experience of handling such tools in his past.

'Once the first one is placed, we have thirty minutes to place the remaining charges before they all explode simultaneously. There's no room for mistakes.'

Black saw Valermos physically gulp when he said this. While he had shown remarkable aptitude since his home was destroyed, he still worried that Valermos may not be up to completing the task. While he would normally have shown frustration towards the Jovian, Black couldn't help but feel a sense of familiarity. Both he and Valermos had lost their worlds to the Voltron, and Black recalled how lost he felt when he first started out in the open universe, fending for himself against an enemy that showed no mercy.

'Valermos, take the elevator down, place your charges on the lower levels, it should be quiet down there.'

The Jovian was about to take his leave when Tom stopped him, uncomfortable about leaving him to fend for himself.

'Be careful down there, remember everything I've taught you.'

Valermos nodded, and the two of them shared a moment to say farewell. Black was instantly reminded of Guard. He had wished every day that he had said goodbye while he still had the chance.

As he watched as the elevator doors close shut, he was unable to unable to ignore the guilty feeling in his gut as Valermos descended through the station to carry out the death sentence he didn't know he'd been given.

'He'll be alright,' Black said, more for his own sake than Tom's.

'Let's just get this over with,' replied Tom as he stepped into the elevator.

'See you on the other side.'

Black was unable to look him in the eye.

When the doors opened, Tom found two Voltron waiting for him. He shot both of them through the head, and quickly dragged their bodies into the elevator to cover his tracks. He was on one of the station's highest levels; from here he could hear the distant sound of machinery, and it didn't take him long to find its source.

All the rooms on the floor were filled with vast factories, lined with hundreds of Voltron all at various points of completion. He had heard tales of whole planets covered in sites such as this, all serving to bolster the enemy's numbers. He shuddered at the thought of how mobile this production facility was. The station could enter the orbit of a planet and overwhelm the occupants below by sheer number alone. He crept into one of the rooms, careful not to cross the lines of production and trigger an alarm. He had to duck as an unfinished torso almost clipped his ears. Crouching down, Tom took one of the charges and attached it to the beam's base.

With one charge placed, he left the room the way he came. He moved across the floor to another room, all the time thinking about how Valermos was faring in the rooms below.

The lower levels were housed with huge engines that fuelled the entire station. Exceptional amounts of energy flowed through the area, and Valermos decided that it was the perfect place to hide one of his bombs.

Black had been right about the lower floors, he hadn't seen a Voltron since leaving the hanger. Because of this his venture down to the level had far easier than he had expected. Of course he was fully aware that this had been intentional, as he knew that Black didn't trust him to fend for himself in the same way that he and Tom could. He was fine with this; however, as he still felt uneasy about confronting the Voltron one on one.

He slipped into one of the rooms and stared up the gargantuan machinery that kept the station running. *A few well-placed charges could bring the station to a standstill,* he thought as he removed one of the explosives from his belt.

'Halt,' shrilled a cold robotic voice.

Valermos leapt out of his skin. He followed the source of the voice to a solitary Voltron, its back to a computer terminal. In that second, everything seemed to stop, and time lost all meaning in his world. As he watched the Voltron raise its weapon, it became evident to him that this was his moment to prove himself.

His gun was in his hand, which came as quite the shock, as he couldn't remember reaching for it. He squeezed the trigger. The beam arced out and caught the Voltron straight through the head. A shower of sparks sprayed all around, and the robot's corpse clunked to the floor. Valermos stared at the fallen Voltron in disbelief, quietly proud of himself. Back on Jupiter a Voltron had almost killed him, if it hadn't been for Tom's timely intervention. Over the last few weeks, he had built up the thought of a second confrontation in his mind until it had made him ill. It was to his immense surprise and relief that the encounter had come and gone with none of the disaster that he had anticipated.

While he was proud of his personal achievement, he knew that he must get back to the task at hand before more Voltron came. He walked over to the terminal where the Voltron had been working and attached one of the charges. He activated the device successfully and gave himself another moment of triumph. The moment was short-lived; however, as he could faintly hear the sound of footsteps echo from the hallway.

Black's path through the space station had been far from stealthy. His anger had kept his blood thirst going, and all along his path were the fallen scraps of metal that were once Voltron. He had reached his third floor now and had placed several explosives across his route. The blast radius of the devices he had planted alone enough to tear the whole upper half of the station apart. His mind wandered to thoughts of the others, and if their imminent sacrifice was needed after all.

His stray thoughts caught him off guard and a sharp pain grazed his left shoulder. Clutching his arm, he rolled, instinctively, raising his weapon to take aim. He found his target - a half-desiccated Voltron that held its weapon shakily in its one remaining hand. Two more blasts whipped past his head and hammered into the featureless wall behind him. He returned the gesture with a shot of his own, that terminated the maimed machine in one swift strike.

Taking solace in the temporary peace, he checked his shoulder. The wound was superficial; the blast had only burned the upper layer of skin. While the wound had the potential to endanger the mission, he was instead thankful that the pain had served to distract him from his troubled thoughts.

He hated the trouble his mind was giving him. He thought back to the days when he travelled alone, where he had no attachments to anyone. The only similar occasion back then was the night he spent with a Voltron agent, but even she hadn't gotten to him this bad.

He grew sick of his troubled thoughts, and tried again to push them to the back of his mind. He removed another of the explosives from his belt and placed it within the deceased Voltron's shattered chest unit. With another explosive placed, he decided that it was time to finish the job he had started. He reached into his pocket and withdrew the detonator, and stroked the trigger with his thumb. By pushing down the button he could end the war in an instant. Without leadership the Voltron Empire would crumble in a matter of months, and the galaxy would be freed from the chains of conflict. He held in his hands the power to save millions, and the only price he need pay was the lives of two innocent souls, caught up in the web that he himself had spun. His conscious wrestled with itself, leaving his body immobilised until a decision was reached. Those thoughts were left hanging when the sound of alarms blared in the distance.

Black could hear the blood pounding in his ears as he sought to trace the source of the alarm. He was filled with a sense of panic, as the fate of the mission and his friends were in jeopardy. As he tangled with which meant more to him, the elevator doors opened, and he found an entire floor crawling with Voltron.

He opened fire and gunned down every Voltron in sight. The robots dropped like flies, offering no opposition. While he stood in the open, an easy target, the enemy simply ran past him. It was then Black realised that the Voltron had been given a more important target: further down the passageway were Valermos and Tom, pinned down under heavy fire. Black smiled, despite himself. He was happy to see his companions, despite their predicament.

More Voltron passed by as they blindly followed orders. Black used this advantage to help his friends, and thinned the Voltron horde with a round of headshots. The advance subsided, and Black saw that Valermos was relieved to see him again.

'Black, thank the Stars!'

The Jovian embraced him in a tight hug, and Black found for the first time in his life that he didn't know how to reciprocate. He patted Valermos awkwardly, yet found warmth in the affection that was given. Seeing that Tom was on edge, Black brought the moment to an end.

'Come on, we better get going.'

The three of them turned to leave, when a voice stopped them in their tracks.

'Don't leave so soon, Captain Black. I've been waiting a long time for this moment.'

The voice grated Black's every nerve, and brought back memories of times he'd long since tried to bury. The flashbacks sought to consume him, and in that moment he recognised the one who had caused them.

'Izak.'

Black turned at was met with the sight of the Voltron leader. Izak towered over his creations, somewhere over seven feet tall, and wore a long cloak that masked the extent of his augmentations. The parts of him that remained were purple and snake-like, and were located primarily on one half of his face. The other side of his face was covered metal; an artificial red eye that shone out at them, watching their every move.

'My spies informed me that you have been trying to locate me. I congratulate you for making it this far.'

'I will never stop hunting you, Izak.'

'Such a predictable motive for an organic: revenge. Pick another one, your pettiness bores me.'

'You destroyed my home, too!' chirped Valermos. 'Jupiter was a peaceful world, worth nothing to anyone.'

'Jupiter held more value than anything in this galaxy, Prince Valermos. My visit to your homeworld was far from unintentional. My greatest regret is that I had to see it destroyed.'

Black growled, the anger he felt rising to uncontrollable levels. It was time he made his choice. The time was now or never.

'It will be the last world you ever destroy.'

He held the detonator up for Izak to see, for him to be aware in his final moments just who had ended his reign. The moment to revel never came, and instead of the horror he expected on the dictator's face, he found that he was laughing.

'You are a desperate fool, Captain Black. The bombs on this station are being disarmed as we speak. My agents have been following your movements for weeks now. I've known of your plans before you even left Earth.' The alien tyrant grinned as he spoke, showing decayed yellow beneath his scaly lips. 'I even know the true motive of your presence here.'

Black gasped, despite himself. *The others can't find out, they just can't.* His heart pounded in his chest as the secret he had kept since leaving Earth was about to be revealed.

'What does he mean, Black?' asked Valermos. Black was unable to meet his gaze.

'Let me tell you, my dear Prince Valermos. You see, Black lied to you: the bombs he had you setting weren't on timers, instead your trusty captain here was planning on destroying this station and everyone on it, including yourselves.'

Izak waited for the bombshell to drop and revelled in the turmoil he'd unleashed. Tom and Valermos exchanged glances, each hoping for some other explanation.

'Black, is this true?'

Instead of protesting and spouting further lies like a coward, Black gave no reply. He felt the hateful gazes from both Tom and Valermos burn into him, right through to his rotten soul.

'You lied to us!'

'We trusted you!'

Black felt broken and defeated as the insults of his former allies came hailing down on him like a shower of stones. He was facing the full consequence of his betrayal, and as a result felt nothing but shame for his actions. It was Valermos that occupied the most of his thoughts; of how he wilfully manipulated his naivety into a weapon for his own motives. His guilt became so much that he wished he had pushed the detonator when the alarms went off.

'Before you came here you believed that you had nothing to lose. How does it feel to lose so much more?

Black remained silent, his mind elsewhere, working on a way to fix the problems he had caused.

'Any last words, Captain?'

'Yeah, sure I do,' he smiled as the rumblings of a plan forming in his mind. 'I was just wondering how many of our explosives your lackeys have found?'

He turned and dived to the floor, pulling Tom and Valermos down with him. Wasting no time, he held out the detonator and pushed down the trigger firmly. There was a distant rumbling, and soon the entire floor began to shake.

'Come on.'

Black heaved the others up and dragged them away. He knew that time was of the essence, and if they were to have any chance of making it out alive, they had to move quickly. Unable to help himself, he spared a glance behind, in the slim hope that a nasty fate had befallen his enemy. He was sickened to see that Izak too had wasted no time in making a dash to safety, his Voltron clearing a path for him through the debris.

He knew his moment had passed, but in a moment of clarity, he had found for himself where his true loyalties lie. With ruthless determination, he pushed himself on; helping the others as they slowly regained their composure. Valermos was first to come round, and fought to pull himself away from Black's supporting hold.

'Who the hell do you think you are?' he said, breaking free of him and stopping the three of them dead in their tracks.

'Valermos, this isn't the time.'

'No, I think it is, Black,' added Tom, also pulling free. 'You took us on a suicide mission without even asking for consent. Why should we go anywhere with you?'

A loud scraping sound interrupted them as something shifted on a floor above. The room once again began to shake, and almost threw the three of them off their feet.

'Right now you don't have much choice.'

Reluctantly, they had to agree, and followed him as he raced down the corridor, heading for their one chance of escape: the *Roc's Feather*.

When they reached the hanger, they found the place to be in a worse state than they imagined. Girders and other support structures hung down from the ceiling, some having sliced through the ships below them. Black's first fear upon seeing a decimated Voltron drop ship was that they would find the *Roc's Feather* in a similar state. The thought haunted him through the graveyard of useless vessels, until the sight of his beautiful blue angel ignited the hope in his heart once more. The site where Tom had landed the ship in the corner of the bay had shielded it from the structural damage. As the place continued to collapse around them, he knew that the ship wouldn't be safe for much longer. He beckoned the others onward and put everything he had into sprinting the last few yards to the ship.

He climbed the landing ramp and felt the relief wash over him. He heard the sound of footsteps behind him as he accessed a nearby panel, taking the ship into emergency autopilot. As the ship lifted off the ground he heard Tom's voice, and from his strained tones he knew instantly that something was wrong.

'Black, it's Valermos!'

He looked down from the ship and saw Valermos. Behind him a tall robot loomed over him, rooting him to the spot in a firm grip. The ship zoomed away and they watched the Jovian shrink into the distance, the hanger falling apart around him.

Chapter 11

Valermos watched as the *Roc's Feather* flew out of the hanger and away from the crumbling Voltron station. He felt sick, as not only had he just lost his only chance of escape, but his friends as well. He had never felt fear like this before. He now knew how it felt to be truly alone. He longed for his lost home; the red skies, the coarse sand, and the arms of a woman he could barely remember.

He felt the cold steel hand of the robot on his shoulder, like Death reminding him that his time had come. The hand held him as tight as a vice, and showed no signs of letting him go. All around the walls were falling in, huge chunks of metal clattering to the ground, closely followed by the contents of the floor above.

He began to wonder why the robot had not yet tried to kill him, not that he was complaining. *Perhaps some Voltron like to gloat*, he postulated. Feeling that there was nothing to lose, he moved his hand down his side, reaching for his pistol. The moment he touched the weapon, the grip on his shoulder tightened. He writhed, the pain far exceeding any threshold he had ever experienced before.

His instinct was to swing himself around to face his attacker. Upon doing so, he smacked his elbow into the robot's arm, loosening its grip for a brief moment. That was all Valermos needed, he broke free and put some distance between himself and the Voltron.

Moving away, he was granted a full look at his attacker for the first time: the Voltron was almost identical to the assassin he had encountered on Vamshi. The robot advanced on him, all armour and hydraulics. Valermos quickly realised that his former tactic of overloading its intelligence wouldn't work here, and he would have to think on his feet if he was to escape alive.

He quickly scanned the room for something to aid him. A broken pipe by his feet made for a makeshift javelin, which he threw with surprising accuracy. The pipe caught the robot in the left shoulder, wedging itself between the rivets where its arm began. The robot pulled the pipe free and threw it to the ground. While the intimidating construct continued to advance, Valermos could see that its left arm hung limp at its side.

Not completely indestructible, then, he thought, a flicker of hope ignited in his soul.

The assassin's continued advance forced him backward, and he took a brief moment to work out where he was going. Behind him, through the falling scraps of building material and girders, was a door, the sign above obstructed by smoke and flame. The exit was his best hope to escape the crumbling hanger, so he had little choice but to take it.

He drew his pistol and fired a succession of shots at the Voltron, focused on its already damaged arm. As expected, the shots caused no damage to its thick armour, but did serve to slow it down.

Valermos utilised his extra time and leapt through the fallen girders. He turned and fired randomly at the supports, and to his glee, the ceiling collapsed further, obstructing the path between himself and the assassin. He made his way through the door, well aware that behind him the robot was trying its best to lift the rubble with its one working hand.

When the doors closed shut behind him, Valermos couldn't believe his luck. The room before him stretched out in front of him like a long corridor, filled either side by rows of escape pods. He immediately ran to the computer console and checked the status of the pods. The display showed that most of the capsules had been launched or damaged. Almost defeated, he couldn't believe his luck when he saw that one pod remained active, located at the end of the bay. He stabbed at the controls to unlock the docking clamps, and saw the hatch open for entry.

Walking down the corridor towards the pod, he couldn't help but notice a tall mass block out the light from behind him. He turned and was instantly greeted by the hand of the assassin reaching out towards him. He ducked to the side, and the hand grasped only air. Backed against the wall, the robot towered above him, blocking out all conventional avenues of escape. He was; however, able to see one chance, albeit a slim one: a two-foot gap between the legs.

Valermos seized the opportunity and dived for the gap, wincing as his armour scraped against the robot's plated legs. He landed on his front and pushed himself along with his elbows, crawling until his legs kicked in and brought him to full height. He saw the pod in front of him, not thirty feet from where he was standing. Before he knew it he was sprinting, his body working overtime to reach a place of safety.

He reached the pod and leapt inside, and not wasting a second he sought out the controls. At the far end of the pod was a computer terminal, the light from the screen acting as a guide for his fatigued limbs to aim towards. Its operating system was simple enough for the Jovian to operate, and he was quickly able to activate the command to close the hatch doors.

Finding a small bunk, Valermos flopped down on the mattress, and felt the tension instantly seep away from every inch of his body. His rest lasted for all but a few seconds, when the sound of the terminal bleeping propelled him into alertness once more. From the bunk he could read the words "hatch malfunction", and didn't have to look far to find where the fault was located.

Through the closing entrance to the pod, the robot was breaking in. It squeezed its way through the gap, all the while resisting the force of the hydraulic doors as they attempted to close. Valermos' heart beat heavily in his chest.

Can't I ever catch a break?

He fired at the Voltron with a burning fury, causing his pistol to overheat as he launched round after round at the maimed menace. He growled at his now useless weapon, yet refused to throw it away as another use for it entered his mind. Walking towards the helpless droid, he grasped his pistol by the barrel, holding it like a hammer to strike at its neck. The blows bashed away this weaker area of the assassin's defences, and exposed the clips where the head was connected to the rest of its body. From here, he was able to disconnect the head, causing the rest of the body to fall limp like a rag doll.

The robot's lower half still hung out of the escape pod, preventing the hatch from closing. With the creature now immobile, Valermos tugged at the machine until it joined him inside.

The pod rumbled as some part of the station crumbled away. Avoiding the scattered remnants of the robot's body, Valermos hopped across the pod to the controls. He punched in the launch commands and the pod released itself from its moorings. After a moment in freefall, the thrusters engaged, pushing the capsule away from the broken station, flames licking at its surface.

The pod drifted across the system, ignored by the streams of Voltron ships escaping the ruins of their former stronghold. As he passed a small moon, a shockwave caught the ship, flinging him against a wall. He ran to the window to see what was happening.

'By the stars!'

He watched with amazement as he witnessed the destruction of the space station. Huge chunks of metal blew outwards from the fiery epicentre, capturing a number of Voltron ships in its wake. He knew he was lucky to have escaped when he did. He'd been lucky for a number of things over the past few hours.

He checked the terminal for a status on his flight path. The guidance system notified him of a habitable planet in range. The information on the world was sparse, yet it was known to hold no indigenous life. While his chances of survival on the planet were slim, he knew he was far better off there than to stay on the pod. He accepted the destination and returned to his bunk, his thoughts solely focused on Tom, and if he would ever see his friend again.

Chapter 12

Black watched, his jaw wide open, as the crumbling Voltron space station faded into the distance. He shut away the outside world became lost in his thoughts. Somewhere on board that station was Valermos, isolated from all help, at the mercy of a lethal Voltron assassin.

Despite the terrible things he had done, he had tried his best to make things right. He believed that getting the others to safety would be a start, but not in a thousand winters could he ever have foreseen the events that came to pass.

While he had already begun the process of punishing himself, Tom had expressed a willingness to help him on his way. His hands grasped him by the collar and slammed him against the wall.

'You left him behind!'

Tom punched him in the gut and he dropped to his knees. Normally his instinct to protect himself would have kicked in by this point, but instead he welcomed the violence, each convulsion of pain acting as penance for the wicked things he had done. Tom continued to attack, and Black felt each perfectly executed blow hammer into his torso. He doubled up on the floor and began to retch.

Tom stared down at him with eyes full of anger, yet couldn't help but feel a sense of pity for the man as he lay in a pathetic heap on the floor. Black was secretly glad of this, as it meant that he ceased his assault, at least for the time being.

'We have to go back there,' Tom said. If there was any form of compassion in his voice, Black could not hear it.

'You know we can't do that.' Tom kicked him again, but Black continued. He wasn't about to embark on another suicide mission. 'It's too dangerous. If we go back there we'll all die. Valermos would never want that.'

Tom snarled.

'You don't get to say his name.'

He lashed out again, but this time, Black was ready. He caught Tom's foot before the blow landed, and yanked it, hard. His centre of balance disrupted, Black continued his assault, delivering a blow to the groin, overbalancing him further. Tom crashed to the ground, knocking the wind out of him. Now at his level, Black climbed on top of him, raising his fist. He beat down on Tom with a cold anger, venting the frustrations of a lifetime with each blow. Tom managed to block the attacks, but Black's unrelenting fury eventually won out, and a bloody fist connected with his face, drawing blood at his lip.

'If left alive, Izak won't stop at Jupiter; he won't even stop when Earth is burned to a cinder. I did what I did to protect every life in this galaxy. While the way I went about it may have been wrong, I refuse to let anyone else go through what I've been through. It was hard enough watching it happen to Valermos...'

He raised his fist for another strike, when a piercing shrill caused him to freeze. The ships alarm was ringing, a severe threat to the ship detected. To further extenuate the noise, something struck the ship. He lowered his fist, drawing his anger back under control, and climbed off Tom.

'Argument over.' He left Tom on the floor as he ran to the bridge. Feeling the sting of defeat, Tom reluctantly agreed. Black had talked about losing his own people, an experience that he and Valermos had both shared. Tom hadn't even begun to realise what that could do to a person, and felt a sense of pity for the man. He wiped the blood from his lip before he followed Black towards the source of the noise.

'We're under attack,' Black announced the moment Tom entered the bridge. He relieved him at the helm and took control of the ships navigation.

'You'd think that destroying their space station would get us off their backs for a bit.' Tom laughed and wished he hadn't. He began to cough uncontrollably, pain arcing out across his body with each spasm. Black could certainly handle himself when the moment was called for.

'You don't know the Voltron like I do.'

There it was: the look of a battle-hardened survivor. It was clear to see that Black had a lot of experience with the Voltron. He shuddered to think the death and destruction he had witnessed firsthand. That kind of trauma made you stop at nothing to tip the scales and set things right. Tom just wished it hadn't have cost him his friend.

'There are two Voltron cruisers on our tail. Taking evasive action.'

He took the ship through a myriad mixture of twists and turns, looping around comets and planets, the enemy craft always close behind. The Voltron fired wildly, hoping that at least one of their shots would find its mark. Tom managed to shield the ship from the attack, placing every astronomical object he could find between them to absorb the blasts. He knew they couldn't last much longer like this without somewhere safe to land to even the playing field. With his free hand he absently fumbled for the scanner, careful not to let his attention drift from his piloting.

'I've scanned the system, but I'm not finding anything helpful.'

'What about beyond the system?'

'We're in the heart of Voltron territory, what do you expect to find, a lost Alliance battle fleet?'

Tom knew Black was feeling bad enough already, but couldn't help but bring him down further.

'I'm not asking for miracles. Just get me away from these damn Voltron!'

He ran the scanner again; a short bleep announced to him that something had been found. The picture showed a small moon at the edge of the system. Environmental information showed that the planetoid had breathable air, laying at the very edge of what their two species considered habitable.

'I've found something, but it's not perfect.'

'It'll do. Take us in.'

The path to the moon was a straightforward flight, but the Voltron didn't plan on making it easy. Fire from their cannons peppered the space around them, boxing them in. The pursuing vessels tailed behind at either side of the *Roc's Feather*, slowly closing the gap between them.

'They're coming in too fast. I don't think I can hold them off for much longer.'

'You better think of something, and quickly.'

'I don't think they'll have thought of this one.'

Tom pulled the brakes on the ship, narrowly avoiding utter obliteration as the Voltron ships both flew past. The fire from the ships refused to cease, creating a corridor of death that spewed from each vessel. Shifting the controls were expert efficiency, Tom darted for the nearest of the ships, hugging as closely to it as possible without collision. The blind fire from the other ship continued to follow its target, ignorant to the fact that it now stood shielded behind its sister. The Voltron ship carved the other wide open, spilling the robotic crew out into the vacuum.

'Nice work!' Black admitted, finding that his hands had been gripping the arms of his chair tightly through the whole fight. 'Now get us out of here before this one finishes the job.'

'Gladly.'

Tom punched the ship into full acceleration, speeding away through the wreckage of the damaged craft. The remaining Voltron vessel sailed after them, its emotionless crew undeterred by the demise of their brethren. With only one ship now after them, the job of evading their attacks became a far simpler job. The path to the moon was clear, and the *Roc's Feather* dived through the atmosphere without stopping. The landscape of the surface was predominantly rocky. Mountainous regions provided much needed cover, yet to navigate them, Tom had to lower their speed. He charted a course for them through the peaks and slopes, dipping and diving as the Voltron continued to fire after them.

'We need somewhere to land,' said Black.

'I'm aware of that,' replied Tom, impatiently.

The end of the mountain range was now in sight. Time was running short if they were to find a way to land in one piece.

'Please tell me that this thing has weapons.'

'Just the forward cannon. I've been meaning to upgrade them for years, but these things just kind of slip through the cracks, you know?'

Tom cursed, knowing the tricky manoeuvre he'd have to pull off if they were to survive.

'Get that cannon, ready,' he said. 'We'll only get one shot at this.'

Black routed the weapon systems to his chair and primed the cannon for action.

'Ready when you are.'

With the final stretch of mountains passing below them, Tom fired his plan into action. He cut the engines, letting the ship freefall through the air. Using the quick shift in momentum, he brought the ship around, so that it faced the pursuing Voltron.

'Now!'

Black fired the cannon, catching the Voltron ship on its side, smoke billowing from the impact zone. The ship began to drop, but managed to fire off one more shot before trailing off into the side of a mountain. The shot caught the spinning *Roc's Feather* in the aft section, just below the engines. A blaring alarm told them the prognosis wasn't good, but that wasn't going to make them give up just yet.

'Damage report!'

'I'm not going to lie to you: we will crash. Let's just see if I can make it as graceful as possible.'

Tom fired up the engines, which put up a fight, giving out short bursts before packing in. He tried again, and a loud roar confirmed that this time it had worked.

The ship was falling sharply, the engines struggling to slow their descent against the ceaseless force of gravity.

'Come on,' he said, pushing the engines to their limit, alert signs popping up all over his console that told him the ship was feeling the strain. Slowly, and remarkably, their descent began to decline. Just fifty feet from the ground, the *Roc's Feather* levelled out. Black and Tom's cheers were so loud they could be heard all about the ship, right through to the hidden room where Guard was sleeping.

'We did it!' Tom said, breathing a sigh of relief.

The ship juddered; their moment of relief short lived. It juddered again, this time followed by the engines shorting, and then cutting out altogether. The ship dropped again, straight down, this time with no wriggle room for saving the fall.

In a large open area of rocky desert, the *Roc's Feather* slammed into the dirt. A shower of dust was thrown into the air, which gently settled on the blue craft, coating it in a brown hue.

'I'll get the repair kit.'

Chapter 13

Vast dunes covered the planet's surface in thick layers of sand. The harsh environment was a challenge for all life that dwelled there, not at least for a solitary Jovian. Valermos' people had once evolved on a world such as this, yet after millennia in the safe comfort of technological advancement, he found that his natural instincts were unrefined, thus survival came as a sharp learning curve.

His escape pod had become his shelter, and with it came the full time job of keeping it above the never ceasing sprinklings of sand that swept across the landscape. Three times a day he covered his face in rags and left the protection of the pod to scout the surrounding area for food. For the problem of hydration, he had managed to recycle moisture from the condensation in the pod's heating systems, accessible once a day after it had carried him through another cold night.

During his stay on the planet, he had little time to pursue any other objective but survival. In the few hours he was able to salvage each day, he set his time to working out a way to escape the nomadic life he had been forced to lead. Sending out a distress call was risky, especially so far into Voltron territory. The chance of finding a nearby Alliance vessel was slim, and dropped even more when it came to finding one willing to enter enemy territory to answer a call from a Voltron escape pod. His only option was to send out an encrypted message, in the hope that a band of scavengers thought he was some lost treasure from a bygone age.

With the task of creating a distress call complete, he had nothing to occupy his time. The nights became lonely, and he longed for the company of others. He missed his friends, and wondered if they were still alive out there.

His mind wandered, picturing them hearing his signal, fantasising about the day they came to the rescue. All thoughts of that died when he remembered what Black had done, the way he had deceived them for so long. The signs had been there all along: since joining the ship, Black had never wanted to interact with them, and only ever talked of their mission.

'That being said, he did help us to escape,' he said out loud, for a moment unaware that he had no audience.

In that moment the loneliness truly sank in. He hadn't spoken to another soul in weeks, and had no idea what he would say if he did. He couldn't live like this for the rest of his life. For a moment he considered removing the encryption on his signal, anything to have a conversation again, even if it was with a Voltron.

While that thought was absurd, it did lead to another, less insane idea. He looked to the remains of the Voltron assassin on the floor, piled in a heap of disembodied limbs and wiring. He thought back to the last assassin he had met, how he had hacked into its memory to locate Izak's space station. That hadn't been too hard, though back then he did have the full resources of the *Roc's Feather* at his disposal. He picked up the head and examined the data entry port on the crown of its skull. It had suffered no damage from the fight, and only a little sand lay crumbled round its edges.

'Let's see if we can bring you back without you trying to kill me.'
Dusting away the sand, he connected the head to the escape pod's computer. A list of alien runes flickered onto the screen – the operating software of the Voltron race. Some characters he recognised from his previous attempt, making the process slightly easier than he had first thought. Decryption software didn't come standard with a Voltron escape pod, but by hacking into pod's own software, he was able to build a rudimentary program in just a few hours.

With the assassin's head undergoing the lengthy process of decryption, the Jovian set about picking up the robot's scattered limbs, reconnecting them to the rest of its body.

If it wasn't for the work on the robot, Valermos knew he would have long since gone insane. The work kept him busy during the long, cold nights, and kept his despairing thoughts at arm's length. Finally, after gargantuan effort, his labours had come to fruition.

The robot stood before him like a knight in armour. Little had changed from its former appearance, save for its visor, which no longer emitted a red light. The robot still held its menacing form, in large part due to its size. Valermos knew it would take him a long time to overcome his instinct to run. The construct had been a trigger of nightmares in the past, and now it was his friend. *Life always throws you a curveball when you least expect it*, he thought to himself.

He tapped at the console and booted up the robot for the first time. His pistol lay ready on the bunk by his side, a precautionary measure in case his skills at reprogramming the robot weren't as sharp as he'd first believed.

The robot's head lifted, slowly, and then began to survey its surroundings. Before conversing with the robot, Valermos leaned to one side, placing his weapon even further within his reach.

'Hello, robot,' he said, suddenly aware that he didn't know how he would converse with it. For a brief moment he wondered whether it was a side effect of his time alone on the planet, and quickly tried to push the doubtful thought aside.

'Greetings, humanoid,' replied the robot.

'You can call me Valermos,' he laughed, despite himself. *At least he doesn't want to kill me.*

'Are you the one who created me?'

'Yes,' he replied, a little too quickly. He decided it best not to divulge the robot's true past right away, not at least until he had done some extensive checks to make sure there wasn't any hiccups left behind in its operating system.

'Then my designation for you must be "Master". My systems indicate that this is the first time that I have been operational. What is my prime directive, my purpose?'

'You are to be my protector, to fight for the Earth Alliance against the Voltron, though, most importantly, you are to be my friend.'

Valermos knew this was a strange thing to ask of a robot, but he knew in his heart that right now he needed a friend, and this was the best choice available.

'Directive accepted, Master, though as an inorganic construct I am unsure how I will be able to function as a friend.'

'Just be there for me when I need you, the rest will work itself out.'

'Affirmative, Master.'

Valermos knew the robot probably still didn't understand friendship. With the right stimulus, it could become anything he wanted. He knew that given time, its programming would adapt to new concepts, and learn just like a child would from its parent.

'Awaiting orders, Master.'

Valermos was taken aback by the request. He had never given an order before. His stomach grumbled, and with it his body gave him the inspiration he needed.

'We need to get off this planet,' he began, his inspiring words completely lost on the robot. 'At the moment we have no ship, and limited food. Until my distress call is answered, pretty much all we can do is sit tight and work on boosting the signal. My time doing that is limited, so the most productive thing you can do for me is to gather food so I don't starve in here.'

'I will search for organic material in the nearby area. Initial scans show that local reptilian life living in the sand is suitable for Jovian dietary requirements.'

With an instruction given, the robot took its leave of him. Before it reached the exit hatch, he thought of something else he wished to tell his new companion.

'Wait!' he called. 'You're name, it's Power Defender. It's the translation of "royal guard" from Jovian.'

'Designation accepted, Master,' the robot replied, before leaving the pod to carry out its mission.

A week passed, and a response to the distress signal had still not been found. Valermos' efforts to boost the escape pod's signal had proved successful, and he was only able to conclude that no friendly ships were in range.

Power Defender had been an invaluable asset, and had kept him sane, despite his limited topics for conversation. His numerous ventures beyond the confines of the pod had brought back valuable materials. At first, he had returned with food, yet given time he was able to find wreckage from derelict spacecraft that had crashed on the planet over the years. While none of the ships had been suitable for spaceflight, the robot had been able to salvage tools and equipment to make his modifications easier.

'Do you think we could modify the pod to be able to achieve space flight?' Valermos asked his companion. The robot had already been programmed with an extensive knowledge of engineering, physics, and a whole range of other topics, all courtesy of the Voltron. If there was a solution to their current situation, Valermos knew that he could rely on Power Defender to help him fix it.

'Based on the current materials I have located so far, it would theoretically be possible to create a propulsion system that would carry the pod out of the atmosphere. The problem from there; however, lies in working out a method of carrying the pod through space.'

'Can't we use the same propulsion system that would get us off the planet?'

'The salvageable propulsion system is from a Draxi reconnaissance probe. Such probes are only intended to work within the confines of an atmosphere, and use oxygen combustion as a means of fuel. The system therefore would be impossible to use in space.'

'It still leaves us with little choice. Let's get the parts of the system we need to start working on it here. In the meantime, scout the area for more ships. There has to be something out there that can get us away from this desolate place.'

'Yes, Master. I shall return shortly.'

The hatch closed and the robot was gone, leaving Valermos alone with his work and his thoughts. With the prospect of leaving a sudden possibility, he started to fantasise about his purpose should he manage to escape the planet. His first thought was to find his friends on the *Roc's Feather*, who were most likely fighting some battle against the Voltron on some far flung alien world. The thought soon faded as, out of nowhere, a burning anger built within him. He had spent over a week on this planet, fending for himself, and his friends had not come for him.

They've left me for dead.

A voice inside told him that it couldn't be true, but part of him wondered, feared that it was.

Perhaps he and Power Defender could strike it out alone, find Izak and finish the mission he had started back on Earth. He had learned much since then, he wouldn't have escaped the space station if he hadn't. Despite his advances, he knew there was still much more to learn. For the time being, he would settle with learning how to build a space craft.

A loud bang from outside jilted him from his thoughts. He ran to his weapon and held it aloft, staying alert to every sound his ears could pick up. For a time, there was nothing, not a single footstep or gust of wind.

'Power Defender?' he called out. It was far too early for his companion return. His last trip into the desert took over six hours. If it was Power Defender, something must have gone wrong; if it wasn't, then something even worse was about to happen.

An idle thought cropped into his mind. He checked the computer, in the vain hope that the noise outside was from a rescue ship. The results on the screen showed that no reply to his broadcasts had been received. Whatever was out there hadn't come to save him.

He continued to listen, and heard a new sound. A faint rustling sound could be heard around the entrance to the pod. He tried to identify what was causing the sound when a hot orange glow appeared around the seams of the hatch.

They're breaking in!

He stumbled back to the other end of the pod, and kept his weapon resting steadily in the direction of the hatch. A line of orange crept around the doorway as the intruders continued to cut their way in. When the line created a neat circle, all the noise stopped and Valermos waited in horror for what came next.

An earth-shattering boom left his ears ringing. He held his hands to his ears in response to the pain that reverberated through his eardrum. A rush of hot air hit him, and the acrid smell of smoke filled his nostrils. In just a few seconds, almost all his senses were left disoriented.

Once his mind adjusted to the confusion, he fought against his senses and regained control. He tried to aim his weapon at the opening, but found that he had dropped it sometime after the hatch exploded. He searched for it frantically, when a figured stepped into the pod. Before he was able to locate his weapon, he felt the barrel of a pistol press against the back of his neck.

'Prince Valermos, my master has been looking for you for a long time,' said Katelyn, before she slammed the weapon against his skull.

Chapter 14

'Damage report,' said Black, nursing a sore head.

The lights were out on the bridge, save for the dim light of the computer consoles dotted around the room. He could see Tom stirring somewhere in front, the sound of his voice having woken him.

'Err,' he replied, getting his bearings. 'The power's out.'

'I can see that. How bad is the damage?'

Black could see him tapping around at his console, and waited impatiently for the results.

'The damage isn't too extensive; there's a few bumps to the forward plating, and one of the fusion circuits has shorted in one main engines. Hull integrity hasn't been breached, that's the main thing.'

'We'll still need to replace that fusion circuit. Any ideas?'

'To be honest, Black, I don't even know what a fusion circuit is. The technology on the *Roc's Feather* is far more advanced than Alliance-tech.'

'My people originally built this ship as a prototype. Over the years I've added numerous additions from the technology of other races. It's surprising how compatible this place is. We just need to scavenge something that will work until we can make proper repairs.'

'Wait a minute,' Tom said, eyeing Black suspiciously. 'You're thinking of scavenging the Voltron ship that chased us, aren't you?'

He looked at Tom as if he what was saying was absurd.

'Voltron ships do come with compatible components, so that's not half a bad idea!'

Tom wasn't having any of it, and saw straight through Black's schemes.

'You were planning this all along, you just wanted to make me think that it was my idea. Admit it, you were, weren't you?'

Black let loose a smile, an admittance that the game was up.

'It's not a bad idea though, is it?'

'You scheming, manipulative bastard.' Tom felt like he could punch him, but held back the urge on this occasion. 'Yes it is a bad idea. The

Voltron on that ship want to kill us, and you want us to walk right to them? It was thinking like this that made us lose Valermos. I thought you'd learn from that, but let's face it, you never will. You won't rest until I'm dead too and you're all on your own.'

'Tom, I-'

'I bet that's what happened to Guard, too.'

Tom said the words without thinking, and instantly regretted them. He felt even worse when he saw the effect they had on Black. The blue-skinned captain screwed his face up into a picture of anger. He had been so reluctant to talk about Guard, even after they found him hidden away inside a cryogenic chamber in the bowels of the ship. He had really touched a nerve this time.

'The day I lost Guard was the worst day of my life. The Voltron tore up my home and my family on the same day. How dare you ever put that on me.'

Black threw a punch, hitting Tom square in the jaw. After all that he had done Tom wanted to hit him back, but seeing the pain in his eyes he decided against it. It was clear to him that both of them had lost someone, and it wasn't fair for either of them to throw insults at each other about it. Tom put aside his anger, and decided to be the better man.

'I'm sorry, Black, I shouldn't have said that. I forgot that you've lost someone too. I miss my friend, that's all.'

Black looked him in the eyes, and forced his temper to cool.

'It's okay. I miss my friend, too. I mentioned the Voltron ship because we have no choice but to go there. If we're going to get off this piece of rock then we have to make repairs. I don't see any other ships out there, so the Voltron one it is.'

'We best get started before they get a jump on us.' He walked over to one of the bridge consoles and tapped at the display. 'The ship went into emergency power upon impact. I'll bring the main power systems back on now.'

Within seconds, all lighting was restored. It took a moment for their eyes to adjust to the bright rays shining down on them from the ceiling. The terminals were now at full power, and Tom had the full complement of the ship's systems to help him locate their target.

'The scanner is picking up a Voltron ship just over the horizon.'

'That's not too far. Grab what we need and let's get going.'

The moon's surface was a harsh environment. Every step they took kicked up a fine dust that blew into their lungs. Tom tore up two lengths of cloth from the shirt he wore beneath his armour, and passed one to Black. By breathing through the cloth, they reduced how much dust they inhaled. Black was thankful, having not thought of the idea himself.

'I'm sorry for the way I've behaved these past months,' he said, staring at the ground. 'It wasn't right, it wasn't *me*. After I lost Guard I thought I didn't have anything left to lose anymore. Meeting you and Valermos has taught me that there is always something to hold on to. My regret is that I saw it only too late. I know Valermos was your friend, Tom, but in the little time that I knew him, he became mine, too.'

Tom saw the haunted look in Black's eyes. He'd been harsh on him since they'd lost Valermos, and rightly so. Until now, he hadn't fully realised that Black had feelings, instead of just some weird alien equivalent. He was showing remorse for what he had done, and any further abuse on the subject would only dig the knife in deeper.

'Valermos wouldn't have wanted us to bicker like we have. Once we get the fusion circuit and get off this rock, let's finish what we set out to do. We put an end to Izak and the Voltron, let Valermos rest in peace knowing that we avenged him.'

Black nodded, and smiled, which was something Tom hadn't seen him do all that often. His smile was warm, a reflection of the man beneath, trying to break free after a lifetime of pain.

'The Voltron ship shouldn't be far, just over this rise.'

Black was right, and, climbing over the next rocky outcrop, they saw the remains of the Voltron ship spread out in the valley below. The wreckage was scattered across a large area, the ship having exploded upon impact. No signs of the craft's inhabitants were anywhere to be seen, which set Tom's nerves on edge.

'Where are all the Voltron?' he asked, eyes darting around the scenery for hidden ambushers or sharpshooters.

'Looking for us no doubt, which means our task here is all the more urgent.'

Together they climbed down into the impact crater and stood amongst the scraps of metal and circuitry strewn that was formerly the Voltron vessel.

'What does a fusion circuit look like?'

'It's a small ball of gases held within a small cylinder of glass. They look quite beautiful, actually, not the sort of thing you'd expect to find in the remains of a Voltron attack ship.'

'Where do you suggest we start looking?'

Black studied the ship's remains for a likely candidate. He pointed to a cone-shaped object protruding from the wreckage that looked to have once been part of the engine.

'The circuit channels the fuel from the engine's reactor to the thrusters. There's a good chance it's still attached to the helix coil at the back of the ignition chamber.'

'You seem to know a lot about Voltron ships.'

'It's always a good idea to know your enemy,' he said as he bent down by the damaged part. He placed his hand into the piece of broken spacecraft and rummaged around inside. Moments later his withdrew his hand, clutching the fusion coil they were seeking.

'Looks to me like you know them too well. Are you sure you're not a Voltron?' Tom laughed, pleased that their stay at the crash site was almost over.

'If that ever happened, you have my permission to shoot me dead,' Black laughed back. 'Come on, we need to get back to the ship before the Voltron find it.'

'After you,' said Tom, following him up the rise and back towards the ship.

A red sun beat down on them as the *Roc's Feather* came into sight. The heat from the star was staggering, and left a glowing heat haze across the landscape. It reminded Tom of the sands of Jupiter, and his days serving the royal family. The haze left the ship the only thing in focus, highlighting its importance like some mystical vision.

Reaching the doors, Black was quick to type in the entry code, allowing the boarding ramp to open and let them into the ship. The door slid open and the ramp began to descend, but Black suddenly paused in front of him, sensing something wasn't right.

'What is it?' Tom asked, but Black failed to reply.

A tingling sensation licked at his neck, and before he was able to turn, a whoosh of heat sent him flying through the air. His head hit the side of the ship, and he felt everything start to fade.

From the floor, he fought against the inevitable, using all his willpower just to stay awake. He saw Black trying to support himself against the boarding ramp, his face covered in cuts. The captain dropped, unable to stay upright despite his protestations. Tom too felt the approaching darkness begin to envelop him. Before his willpower finally gave out, he felt a cold hand touch him, and the smell of oil fill his nostrils. Everything after that was blackness.

The choking sensation of dust in his lungs was the first thing Tom was aware of. He heaved and coughed until his chest hurt, and then his brain finally caught up with what had happened.

He was tied to a rock, Black beside him. A squad of battered Voltron soldiers pointed their weapons at them, ready to fire at the slightest hint of escape.

It had been an ambush!

His thoughts began to race, realising that had been the reason why they had found no signs of the Voltron near their ship. While the robots were typically mindless drones, they were cunning when the need for it came.

'Commander, the organics have awoken,' one of the Voltron announced to its superior.

Tom identified the officer in question, and was horrified by the sight before him. The Commander was formerly human, though the modifications to his physiognomy were shocking to witness. A metal skull had been grafted to the side of its head, and a number of other mechanical augmentations were located throughout its entire left side. The Human hand that hung from his arm was blue, as though all the life that once existed there had long since abandoned ship. The Voltron Commander was nothing short of a walking corpse, more machine than anything remotely resembling the Human it once was.

'Which of you identifies as the Jovian; Valermos?' asked the Commander, its voice absent of any emotion.

'He's dead,' replied Tom, spitting the words from his mouth like poison.

'Verification will be required,' he turned to his subordinates. 'Search the ship, leave no place unchecked.'

'Stay out of my ship, you heap of shrapnel,' Black shouted with barred teeth. Ignoring his futile protest, the Voltron entered formation at the foot of the boarding ramp, and entered the ship as one.

The Voltron swarmed the ship like locusts, filing out into every room they came across. The mindless drones followed their orders and searched each room, looking for any signs of life. They travelled deeper into the vessel, towards the bridge, leaving no stone unturned. Alarms blared when the motion sensors detected the Voltron running through the corridors, calling out for help that was unable to respond.

In a dark room, deep within the depths of the ship, a red light flashed on a cylindrical pod. An intermittent bleep indicated that a change had occurred in the interior of the capsule. The glass window of the pod was shrouded with a thick mist, which slowly began to clear with a hiss of air. As the freezing smoke left the pod, the temperature rose to levels more comfortable for its occupant. The lid of the capsule slid open with a clunk, and for a moment all within the room was still. That was until a hand emerged from the pod, grasping the side tightly.

Outside the ship all was quiet, as the Voltron Commander waited in silence for his drones to carry out their task.

Tom felt frustrated at the hopelessness of their situation. He looked over to his weapon, which lay by the Commander's feet, wishing that it lay within even stretching reach of where he was being held.

'You'll find nothing inside,' he said, the only thing he really could do in the situation.

'If the Jovian is not found, then you will die.'

'Well then it looks like we're goners,' said Black, tugging hopelessly at his bonds.

'Why are you after Valermos, anyway? Aren't we good enough for you?'

'Lord Izak has plans for the Jovian.'

'What kind of plans?'

'That information is classified.'

'Your plans are ruined before they even begun. Didn't you hear me? Valermos is dead!'

The Commander turned its back on its prisoners, effectively stonewalling any further questioning. Raising its right arm, it began talking into a communicator implanted into its wrist.

'Report: have you located the Jovian?'

All that came from the other end of the channel was static. Checking that the device was working, the Commander leaned in to ask again.

'Report your status.'

Again the line was dead. For a moment Tom thought he heard frustration in the cyborg's voice.

'Check what's going on inside,' the Commander barked to the soldiers closest to him. Obeying their orders without question, the four soldiers grouped together and headed up the boarding ramp and into the ship. Seconds later, the soldiers were propelled out of the ship with great force. They slammed into the ground, sparks crackling from their broken bodies.

'Shoot on sight,' the Commander shouted. 'Do not stop until the hostile is eliminated.'

The Commander and its remaining soldiers raised their laser rifles towards the ship's entrance. They didn't need to wait long until an unidentified male dived out from the ship with great speed and rolled down the boarding ramp. He fired shots from a Voltron rifle the moment he left the ship. Each shot fired hit its target with remarkable accuracy, until all that remained was their Commander.

The Commander continued to fire at the newcomer with no intention of stopping. The man avoided each shot with remarkable agility. Stopping behind a small rock, he unpinned a grenade and threw it in the Commander's direction. The projectile exploded on impact, scattering the splintered shards of the Voltron officer in all directions. When the smoke cleared, Black found himself looking upon a face he hadn't seen since he first fled his homeworld; a face he thought that he would never see again.

'Guard...'

Black held an expression of pure shock on his face. He tugged at his bonds, trying to free himself so as to embrace his old friend. Guard regarded him curiously, lowering his weapon.

'I woke from the pod and saw Voltron all around.' His voice was distant, confused.

'The Voltron ambushed us and boarded the ship,' explained Tom. 'If you hadn't have woken, we'd be dead by now.'

Guard nodded, and set about freeing them. He untied Tom's bonds first, and then moved on to Black.

'It's good to see you again, old friend.'

This seemed to shock Guard, who stopped partway through untying his old friend. It was Black who looked more shocked, as the truth dawned on him in a moment of horror.

'Don't you remember who I am?'

Guard stared at him, attempting to draw at the memories in his head, to put a name to the face he found so familiar.

'Maybe it's a side effect of the stasis pod?' suggested Tom.

'When he was shot the weapon caused some neural damage. I thought the pod would have fixed that.'

'The mind is a tricky thing, Black. Time seems to be the only thing that truly fixes it.'

'I remember some things,' announced Guard, scratching his head.

Pulling his hands away, he stared at them, as though looking at them for the first time. 'Were my hands always this colour?' he asked, noting the pinkish hue they seemed to have developed since he last saw them.

'They were once blue, like mine,' admitted Black. 'Valermos and Tom donated their DNA to start the regeneration in your cells. It looks like they passed along some other things, too.'

'It would also explain the strength,' added Tom, recalling the way he had dispatched an entire squad of Voltron single-handed.

'Not to mention the reflexes,' Black agreed. 'You were always the better fighter, old friend, but you were never *that* good.'

Guard continued to stare down at himself, a look of concern spread across his face.

'I'm not the same person at all, am I?'

Neither Black nor Tom knew what to say. It was clear Black still saw the same man in front of him, despite the differences in his biology. Guard; however, was clearly having problems coming to terms with the changes.

'I remember...' he said, gently. 'Tsan, the day the Voltron invaded.'

'And?' asked Black, a spark of hope igniting in his soul.

'They came as friends, but they lied. Our whole world fell to Izak and his fleet.' He paused as another memory entered his mind. 'I also remember the promise you made that day.'

'I told you I would never give up; never stop until I found a way to heal you.'

'You always kept your word, old friend.'

'Are we talking about the same person here?' asked Tom, not sure himself if he was joking or not.

'Black is the greatest friend I have ever known,' Guard said, raising his voice. 'His honour is without question, and he would stop at nothing to do what's right.'

Tom felt intimidated by Guard. His domineering physique and angered tone made him feel inferior in comparison. He was certainly not a man to be trifled with lightly.

'Tom's right, Guard,' Black chirped up to calm him down. 'Things haven't been easy since Tsan. I've made some choices over the years that I'm not exactly proud of.'

'Somewhere along the lines you may have lost your way, my friend, but I still see the man I knew. You look like you've fought hard these past years. Did you manage to defeat Izak?'

'We managed to find Izak aboard a hidden space station just a short time ago, but we failed to destroy it before he escaped. We lost Valermos on board the station when it went down, all because of my stupid plans.'

'Valermos was the other one who helped heal me, wasn't he?'

Black nodded and held his head low, not wanting to revisit the memory of seeing his Jovian friend stood alone on the station while the whole place came caving in around him.

'Valermos lost his people to the Voltron, too,' said Tom. 'He and I joined the *Roc's Feather* to kill Izak and end this war.'

'It looks like we've all lost someone to the Voltron. I've missed a hell of a lot being in stasis, and a lot of things have changed. One thing I do know is that I'm always ready for a fight, and at the very least I owe Valermos a debt of gratitude for helping to bring me back to fight it.'

'There's a lot we need to consider before we jump straight back into the fight. The ship still needs some thorough repairs, and we're too far out to seek help from the Alliance.'

'I know a place that's not far from here that's safe,' said Black as he climbed on the boarding ramp to the ship. 'It should give us just the time we need to get back on our feet.'

'Let's get going,' said Guard. He still felt the adrenaline in his body from his fight with the Voltron, and never was one to stay in one place for too long.

'Tom, are you with us?'

He stared up at Black, who extended a hand to him in friendship. Despite his initial distrust of the Tsani captain, he'd seen a noticeable change in his demeanour since they had lost Valermos, which he hoped was for the better. He knew it was time to drop his grudge, and continue on, in the name of the friend he had lost. He grasped Black's hand and joined him aboard the *Roc's Feather*.

'I'm in.'

Chapter 15

Rays from the hot desert sun licked at Valermos' skin, bringing him back to the conscious world. His head throbbed with pain, and he could feel a trickle of blood seep from the wound.

He was being dragged through the sand by a Voltron, its silver fist clamped round his collar like a vice. He craned his neck around and saw two more Voltron. In front of them walked another figure, though she was far from Voltron: long, dark hair swept down her back, ending in a point at her hips. At first Valermos thought she was another prisoner, until he saw that, unlike him, the Voltron appeared to follow her as though she was their superior.

'The Jovian is awake,' announced one of the Voltron. The female dropped back and came into view. She was attractive, Valermos thought, which made it all the more a shame that she was an enemy. She stooped down to his level and began to study him, as though he was a hamster trapped in a cage.

'There is no lasting damage,' she said, quite lifelessly, and started to examine his head more closely. 'He appears fit for Lord Izak's purposes.'

'What do you mean, "Izak's purposes?"' he asked, beginning to feel uneasy.

'You are to be transferred to a facility on the planet Pridon.'

'And what will happen to me there?' Valermos yelped, beginning to struggle against the grip of his jailor.

'That information is unknown,' she replied, for a moment almost sounding like a Voltron. The news did nothing to settle his nerves. He studied her for a moment, and more questions began to stack up in his mind.

'I didn't know that people worked for the Voltron. I thought Izak hated all organic life.'

'Izak has organic agents spread throughout the galaxy. We serve a number of functions for him.'

'Until you don't.' The statement didn't seem to concern the woman, and made Valermos more curious as to just who she was. 'What's your name?'

'My name is Agent Katelyn. I have served with the Voltron for three solar rotations.' The words spilled from her mouth like an involuntary reflex. If Valermos was right, there was more to this Voltron agent than met the eye.

'Has *Agent* Katelyn, always been your name, or did it just used to be "Katelyn?"'

'Your organic humour is wasted on me, I-'

The Voltron holding Valermos stumbled, its foot hitting something buried just beneath the surface of the sand. The interruption was enough for the Voltron to loosen its grip on him; just enough for him to pull himself free and escape. He wasted no time in doing so, breaking into a roll and sprinting away from the three Voltron and their commander. One of the Voltron raised its rifle to shoot him, but Katelyn quickly stopped it.

'No,' she snapped. 'Lord Izak needs the Jovian alive!'

The Voltron followed in quick pursuit, their mechanical bodies unencumbered by the heat. The Voltron, on the other hand, struggled with the sand. Their feet were rigid lumps of metal, and were unable to adapt to the shifting sand like Valermos.

He continued to run, not even knowing where he could run to. The escape pod he formerly called home couldn't be seen from his current position, and he knew that the Voltron would only find him again even if he ever was to make it back there. He thought to Power Defender's fate; had the Voltron dealt with him before they found his escape pod, or did they simply not know he existed? As his lungs began to burn with exhaustion, he hoped for the latter.

Nothing but sand could be seen for miles around. He knew that before long the Voltron would reach him and he would be recaptured. For just a second, he thought he caught sight of something that dipped behind one of the dunes: a shadowy figure, clad entirely in black.

106

'Power Defender!' he shouted, not sure if what he'd seen was real or just a mirage.

'Power Defender!' he called again, but nothing emerged from behind the dune.

He stood there hopeless, realising his last chance of escape rested solely on a figment of his imagination. Once more, the lifeless hands of the Voltron grabbed him from all sides, exterminating all the hope left in his desperate soul.

He screamed until his throat hurt, yelling out to the desert sun, praying for anything to save him from the life laid out before him.

'Quiet yourself, Jovian. Lord Izak will decide your fate now.'

Refusing to go quietly, Valermos was dragged, kicking and screaming, all the way to the Voltron ship. All that remained of his presence was the single line of his trail in the sand.

Chapter 16

'When you said you knew a place that was safe, this wasn't what I had in mind.'

Tom looked around the bar with a definite sense of disgust. Places like this were the reason the Earth Alliance had rules on conduct outside working hours. The place was crawling with the scum of at least a dozen species, almost all of them up to something at least one of their governments would deem illegal.

A bottle zipped past Tom's head and smashed on the wall behind him. 'When I said that, I meant a place safe from the Voltron. Do you really think they'd ever come here?'

Ignoring Tom's near-brush with injury, Black strode towards the bar, Guard closely following behind. The bartender was a stout Draxi. A deep scar ran down the left side of her brown, wrinkled face.

'Nice to see you again, Black. What can I get you?' She had a deep voice, which seemed at odds with her stature.

'You too, Grog. Three bottles of Antarian whiskey, please. I'm surprised you remember me, it's been a while since I last visited these parts.'

'I remember everyone who visits my bar, especially a Tsani. You're an endangered species, you know.'

'All too well,' he replied, with a little more attitude than he intended. Grog ignored this, realising that she had overstepped the mark, and left to get their drinks.

'So you've been here before?' asked Guard.

'A while back now, before I joined the Alliance. I got into a fight with a couple of Menith over who bought the next round.'

'From what I recall, it was a fight you started,' said Grog, passing him their drinks.

'Yeah probably, my memory's not entirely clear on the subject. But I did save this whole place from a passing Voltron patrol the next day.' He picked up the drinks and picked out a table.

'You've lived a whole life since I last saw you. There's so much that I've missed.' Guard looked disheartened when he heard tales of Black's exploits. Tom knew that if he had shared in his friend's experiences, they would have most likely changed him like they did Black. He often wondered how Valermos would have dealt with the problems they had faced since the space station. Those thoughts made him miss his friend all the more.

'Now is the time to make up for those times.'

Black found a table and placed the drinks down. A Pucian at the next table eyed them suspiciously as they sat down. Guard met his gaze with an intimidating stare, and the long-limbed alien shifted his attention to his drink.

Tom took a sip from the bottle and almost gagged as the fiery liquid scorched his insides. Whatever Antarian whiskey was, it was far from the stuff he used to drink back on Earth. Black and Guard seemed to have no problems with the spirit, and each downed almost a third of the bottle in one gulp.

'So, down to business.' Black sat his drink back down on the table.

'I don't even know the state of the galaxy these days,' said Guard. 'How are the Draxi and the Xiz faring against the Voltron?'

'The Draxi have all but given up fighting. Their trade routes into this part of the galaxy have almost frozen up altogether. The Xiz, as usual are being all mysterious and refuse to get involved, though Izak knows better to antagonise them.'

'So we're effectively alone. What about this Alliance you're working for, don't they have a fleet to help us?'

'The Alliance fleet is far smaller than it used to be. It can barely protect its own territory from the Voltron. I doubt any of the admirals would risk withdrawing from the outer systems.' Tom held the Alliance in the highest regard, but even he accepted that they had limits. It had been several years since the early skirmishes against the Voltron in the Unknown Regions, and many Alliance ships had been lost. He sympathised with them not wanting to risk such losses again.

'Smaller races like the Tetrips and the Pucians won't dare put up a fight. They're just living on borrowed time until the Voltron strike their worlds next.'

The Pucian at the next table notably shifted at the mention of his species, moving in to listen closer. Guard noticed this movement, and rose from his seat.

'Go back to your drink. We don't like eavesdroppers on this table.'

'We don't like Humans in these parts, either,' replied the Pucian.

Guard, insulted to be mistaken for another species, forgot for a moment about the recent change to his skin colour. In a moment of rage, he tossed his chair aside with a remarkable feat of strength, and advanced on the Pucian. The intoxicated alien, unable to perceive the obvious futility, threw up his long arms and readied himself for a fight. Guard grabbed one of the limbs and snapped it with the flick of his wrist. The Pucian dropped to the floor, clutching his forearm.

'I know he has a lot to deal with at the moment, but this...' Tom watched the events occurring with his jaw open, struggling to believe what had happened.

Black ran over to his friend and stood between him and the helpless alien at his feet.

'Guard, calm down. The guy was out of order, but he didn't deserve that.'

Guard grunted, allowing his anger to dissipate before replying.

'Sorry, Black, I couldn't help it. I just feel so angry. The Voltron took my home, years of my life, and I haven't been able to anything about it.'

'Beating up barflies isn't the way to go about sorting it.'

'I think it's time we left.' Tom interrupted; pointing out the mixed looks they were getting from the bar's other occupants.

'I brought us here because this bar is a meeting place for snitches and crooks of all races. If there's some rumour of Izak's whereabouts, we're finding it before we leave.'

Black, ignoring the unwelcome looks, walked back to the bar. Grog waited for him, not looking too pleased with him.

'Do you mind telling me what are you boys really doing here? Beating up my customers better not be your answer.'

'Sorry for the mess, Grog, I'll pay for the damages. We're here looking for news on Izak, either his whereabouts or what the hell he is planning. Know anyone who could help us out?'

'Talk to Ivan over there. He just came back from trafficking a group of Menith from Claros.'

'Much appreciated, Grog. I'll see you around.'

He threw bunch of notes down on the counter, and the three of them headed straight for the scruffy-looking Human she was pointing to.

'Not too soon, I hope.'

Ivan barely seemed to notice them as they approached, at odds with everyone else in the vicinity, who could scarcely keep their eyes off them.

'I heard you have some news on Izak.'

Ivan regarded Black for a moment, and then proceeded to take a sip of his drink.

'My friend asked you a question,' snapped Guard, moving in to rough him up. Black held up a hand to stop him.

'Your pet has quite the temper,' Ivan said, finally. 'He could get you into trouble.'

'You seem to get in plenty of trouble yourself,' said Tom. 'People trafficking is quite the occupation.'

'Just a little job to pay the bills,' he replied, smugly.

'Do any of them involve the Voltron?'

'I'm not foolish enough to work for them, but our paths have crossed from time to time.'

'Then it seems we might both benefit from them being removed from the playing field. Tell me what you know and I'll make it worth your time.' Black removed another wad of notes from his pocket and wafted them in front of the smuggler's face, which seemed to grab his attention.

'I heard he's looking for Poseidon. Why he would be doing that, I don't know.'

'Thanks for your time,' said Black, and threw the money on the table in front of him.

'You be careful out there, Captain. I'm sure you've heard the stories of Poseidon. They're far from pleasant.'

'We can take care of ourselves,' Black replied, taking leave of the smuggler, and his friends with him.

'Poseidon; does he mean the Greek god?' Tom asked, incredulously.

'Surely he can't be serious, Black?' said Guard, ignoring Tom's question entirely. 'I thought those stories were just fairy tales?'

'I guess we find out.'

Silence followed them as they left the bar. When the doors shut behind them, the stares and silent whispers ceased. Within seconds they were forgotten and the rowdy atmosphere of the bar resumed, and for a moment, Grog wished they'd never left.

Chapter 17

The bonds tying Valermos' hands together were excruciatingly tight. That, coupled with them permanently fixed above his head made the pain almost unbearable.

He had lost count of the days he had been here, the lack of any kind of window made the passing of time almost impossible to gauge.

His cell was a sorry affair: no bed, no sink, and just a bucket beneath him to catch any bodily waste. Despite this being a Voltron prison, his surroundings were grimy. Thick mould grew on every wall, threatening to create an entire ecosystem of its own, especially when coupled with the flies that frequented his bucket.

He hadn't seen another soul in... well he wasn't quite sure of that, but it had been a while. He didn't count the Voltron who came to feed him in that; their limited understanding of how fast a person could eat had earned them that.

Before he was brought here, the Voltron agent had told him Izak had some kind of plans for him. If it wasn't rotting away in a damp, cold cell, he was at a loss to think of what it could be.

The door to the cell opened with a clunk and a nerve-shattering creak. Two armed Voltron entered, though he struggled to think why they needed to be armed, he wasn't exactly combat ready. The door remained open, which was unusual, though it did allow him a glimpse of the room beyond the door. The rare glance of a white wall was the only excitement he had enjoyed since he had arrived.

Another figure entered the cell, someone Valermos had anticipated a visit from since he arrived.

'Prince Valermos,' Izak boomed. 'I'm so pleased that we have this opportunity to converse. Our last meeting on board my space station ended rather abruptly.'

'Yes, when we tried to kill you. Shame it didn't work.' After a lengthy time in solitary confinement, Valermos was thrilled to have remained so sharp.

'Captain Black has hunted me for years. I suspected foul play from the moment you were detected on board. Escape was a simple measure.'

'You seem quite the survivalist.'

'As do you, my Jovian friend. Do you realise how much trouble I have gone through to get you here? The moment you left Earth I sent my finest Voltron assassins to collect you. After they both failed in their task, I then had to resort to Agent Katelyn to get the job done. It insults me that an organic agent succeeded where my Voltron failed.'

'You should build better servants,' he laughed.

Izak smiled, and began to regard one of the Voltron that occupied the room with him.

'Do you know why I created the Voltron, Valermos?'

'Enlighten me,' he said, in a tone that suggested he didn't care. In truth, he was fascinated to learn how and why the most ruthless killing machines in living memory had been conceived.

'My people once belonged to a great Alliance of Systems. We were the runt of the litter, frowned upon by all the other races. We were kept around for our minds, though as I'm sure you are aware, the mind is the greatest weapon of all. I delved into the ancient records and found an entry for a former member of the Alliance called the Jovox. The Jovox were a weak species, and therefore relied on artificial constructs for conquest and expansion. The Alliance of Systems became fearful of the Jovox's power, and rallied their forces to destroy them. A law was then passed banning the creation of any form of artificial intelligence.'

'I would imagine that you were never one for the rules?'

'Quite,' he smiled. 'The record system contained detailed information about the construction of their dreaded battle droids, a simple oversight that would cost them dearly. I utilised the designs and created what later became known as the Voltron. Under my direction, the Voltron overthrew the ruling races, and my people reigned supreme.'

'But what happened to them, your people? I don't see them sharing in your glory.'

'They were a hindrance. They failed to see my greater vision for the galaxy, so I had them exterminated.'

'You really are a psychopath, aren't you?' Valermos glared at the vile dictator with utter contempt. His people were only one of many races crushed by the Voltron, how many more before this was all over?

'Thank you for your narrow-minded diagnosis, but like all others, you misunderstand my ultimate goals for the universe.'

'Which are what?'

Izak smiled that repulsive grin that carried all the wickedness that lay within.

'Why, Prince Valermos, the eradication of life, of course.' He laughed, which sounded like the chorus of hell itself. 'Life is a cancer. It spreads throughout creation destroying all in its path, yet ultimately, nothing lasts forever. I plan to outlast it all, but in order to do that, I first need to eradicate the unpredictable variables.'

'Is that what you see people as, just variables in a grand experiment?'

'Sentient life exists on the basis of free will. Where they are loyal one day, the next they could just as easily stab you in the back. I find my Voltron much safer to have around than any organic.'

Valermos wriggled uncomfortably in his restraints, and felt a shock of pain course through his arms.

'If you are perfectly happy in the company of your mindless death machines, then why are you keeping me here? Surely it suits your ends better to have me killed then locking me up.'

Izak smiled again, and licked his lips in delight.

'You are an intelligent one.' He stalked close to him, stroking at the Jovian's red flesh with his gauntleted hand. 'Over the decades I have conquered many races, all stepping stones on the path to my ultimate victory. Your people were the latest, though my reasons for that particular extinction were just the first step of my latest stratagem.'

'My people were no threat to anyone. We were peaceful, nomads in fact.'

'But they were once so much more,' he exclaimed, excitement building within him. 'Were you aware that the Jovian Empire was once one of the greatest civilisations in the galaxy? There was a time when they once rivalled even the Xiz.'

'That was a long time ago,' Valermos whispered. 'The war with the Terrovore changed all that. Both sides of the War lost everything, and just a handful of Jovians remained the only survivors.'

'Were you aware that they once attempted to rebuild? Huge devices were sent out into space, built to reprogram the atmospherics of entire planets.'

'I've heard the stories. Huge arks filled with Jovian colonists were sent out after them. They were just fables, stories to keep a broken civilisation from tearing itself apart from within.'

'Not entirely a fable,' said Izak, matter-of-factly. 'I have found one of the legendary Jovian terraformers.'

Valermos couldn't believe what he was hearing. He knew Izak was insane, but believing fairytale to be fact took things a tad too far.

'All Jovian technology was destroyed when the War ended. My people simply didn't have the resources to build terraformers, let alone send them out into space.'

'Yet I have one in my possession, salvaged from a remote world on the fringes of our galaxy. As we speak, my agents are working to rebuild it, repurposing it for my own goals.

'What use do you have with terraforming technology? Voltron can survive in almost any environment.'

'You're still thinking in limited terms. While terraforming can be used to make desolate worlds habitable, they can also be used to make occupied worlds entirely inhospitable.'

'You're a monster.' Valermos was disgusted. He spat at the Voltron leader, a gesture worthy of vermin on a thousand worlds, yet never before expressed so succinctly.

'That brings me to you, my dear prince. I attacked your world to find a way to work the device, sending my forces down to the planet to gather as much intelligence as possible on the workings of Jovian technology. When the Alliance interfered with my plan I was forced to destroy your people's precious Atmos-Sphere and wipe Jupiter from existence, but not before learning just what it was I needed.'

'Which is?' Valermos snapped, tired of the endless ranting which Izak seemed to enjoy.

'I need you; though more specifically, your DNA. You see Jovian technology works primarily on the premise that no other life form than a Jovian should be using it. By having my own pet Jovian, the device will be mine to control.'

'You do realise that will never happen. You destroy my planet, my people and have probably killed my friends too. There's no way I will ever serve you.'

'Oh, you innocent child, I don't need your permission. My creations are hardly known for their ethical conduct, after all. I just need you alive.' He beckoned to one of his bodyguards, who brandished a long syringe. The needle pushed into Valermos' abdomen and extracted a large sample of blood.

'When my plans are complete, my repurposed device will be sent to Earth. Imagine; the heart of the Earth Alliance, torn apart until nothing remains.'

'You're a monster, Izak, a vile creature who delights in chaos.'

'I prefer to think of myself as a surgeon, who takes pride in healing the universe of its disease.'

'While the rest of the universe thinks of you as a foul little child who likes to play god.'

Izak smiled and turned his back on the Jovian, tiring of their conversation.

'In the morning a ship will arrive to transport you to the secure location where the device is currently housed. There we will harvest as much genetic material as required until the weapon is ready for deployment. Rest up, my prince, for tomorrow you finally get to meet your destiny.'

Laughing, Izak left the room. The two bodyguards followed after him and made sure that the door was once again sealed. As he hung there in the darkness, he could still hear Izak's cackles in the distance.

When the sounds stopped, Valermos thought over what Izak had said. If his plans were carried out, he would be the one truly responsible for the death of billions. Despite this, he knew that there was nothing he could do. He contemplated killing himself, the one sure way to stop Izak's plan stone dead. As another sharp pain coursed through the nerves in his arms, he knew that suicide wasn't possible even if he wanted to.

As the realisation dawned on him that there was truly nothing he could do, he resorted to the one thing that was left: he cried. His sobbing echoed off the walls of his cell, a cruel mockery that only made things worse. He prayed for a miracle, for his friends to find him; for the Alliance to discover where he was and take the whole place out in a carpet bombing.

He closed his eyes and began to listen; wishing that some sound in the corridor might give him some hope of escape. He fantasised about Tom kicking down the door, a squad of Alliance soldiers behind him, or some other band of resistance come to free all those imprisoned alongside him.

He heard something at the door, a scuffling sound as something played with the lock. His heart pounded in his chest, wondering if perhaps his dreams were coming true, or if the Voltron had just come to take more samples.

When the door finally did open, he found what lay on the other side something else entirely.

Chapter 18

'I remember the stories of Poseidon all too well,' said Black as he stared from his chair into the dark depths of space. 'The ancient god of the stars, tyrant of the Seven Systems.'

'That's not the story of Poseidon on Earth,' explained Tom. 'The Poseidon of ancient Greek mythology ruled the oceans of the world, one of many gods, in fact.'

Guard rose from Valermos' old seat by the weapons system and went to join Black looking out at the stars. 'Let's hope that there aren't any more of them out there.'

'The stories of Poseidon are present on a number of worlds, Tom, each with their own interpretation. Were there ships in the stories of Earth?'

'Yeah, lots in fact. Poseidon would often attack unwary ships that dared sail into his waters.'

'Did you ever stop to think that those unwary ships might have been star ships; that Poseidon's waters might actually have been star systems that belonged to him?'

Tom laughed, what Black was suggesting sounded ridiculous to him. 'The stories of Poseidon on Earth were told thousands of years ago. Humans didn't develop interstellar travel until the late 21st century!'

'You'd be surprised by how many worlds out there have had their history influenced by alien culture at some point or another.'

'Poseidon came to our world around the time we developed space travel,' explained Guard. 'He warned our first space travellers that if we were to ever venture into his territory, then he would unleash a fury on our world like we had never seen before.'

'Naturally we took his advice,' added Black.

'So where is his supposed area of space?' Tom was still sceptical. He had been raised in an era of pure logical thinking; the superstitious times of ancient Earth were far behind his "enlightened" realm of thought.

'The Tartarus system.'

'The ancient Greek underworld...' he whispered. *Perhaps the stories were true.*

'The legends state that any ship entering the system never returns. It's the age-old terror story of the galaxy.' Guard seemed cautious when he spoke, the stories engrained in him since childhood.

'So we're going planning on going in there?'

'If Izak is seeking to recruit Poseidon, we need to stop him.' Black was deathly serious. Tom already knew the man would go to great lengths to stop him, and it seemed that becoming part this horror story was no different.

'Suppose we just let the Voltron enter the system. They might succumb to the same fate.' Even though Tom wasn't keen on the idea, he knew he had a point.

'It's too risky,' said Guard. 'We can't leave things to chance. We need to go in there and sort things out ourselves, even if that means killing Poseidon too.'

'So we're into God-killing now? I think we're in way over our heads here. We need to call the Alliance.'

'We're too far from Alliance space,' said Black. 'Even if we weren't, they've got enough problems of their own with the Voltron. It's settled: we travel to the Tartarus system and find out what's going on.'

'I've got a bad feeling about this...'

'Black's right, Tom, we're on our own in this.'

Tom had to agree. Who knew what was happening back home. For all he knew, Earth could be under attack right now. Out here they had a chance at fighting the enemy behind their own lines, where each blow was more devastating than any delivered on the frontline.

He plotted a course for the Tartarus system, and felt the ship's engines kick in, sending them into the darkest frontier they had yet encountered.

All three of them were uneasy when the ship entered the system. If the stories hadn't been enough to assuage them, the derelict ships floating dead in space were certainly enough to set them all on edge. 'Is anyone still in doubt that the stories weren't true?' asked Guard. His attempt at humour fell flat, as the others were still taking in the damage that had been dealt to the derelicts.

'That one's a Xiz saucer.' Tom pointed to a disk-shaped craft to their left. 'I never thought I'd see one, let alone a destroyed one. An entire fleet would have trouble defeating just one Xiz ship.'

'This is bad,' said Black. 'Some of the ships here don't even look that old.'

'Is there any chance of us heading back?' Tom hadn't been keen on the idea of meeting a vengeful god from the outset. A spaceship graveyard was one step too far for him.

'Do you really think we can let the Voltron recruit an ally like this? With an ally like Poseidon, every civilisation in this galaxy is toast. At least at the moment we have a little hope.'

'Guard's right, Tom; I don't like it anymore than you do, but we have to stop the Voltron now before things get a lot worse.'

In his years working for the Alliance Tom had fought battles where the enemy had them outnumbered by impossible odds, but he had come out the other side more or less in one piece. He struggled to understand why this time he was having so much trouble casting his fears aside. Despite this, he conceded, knowing that they had to do something before events escalated into something they couldn't control.

'Just for the record, I really don't like this.' He tried his best to force his emotions into check, pushing his thoughts into finding the location of Poseidon's planet. 'I'll try to get the scanners to push through the wreckage. There must be a planet in there somewhere.'

The task would prove harder to than he first thought. The sheer amount of broken vessels was staggering. It became a full time task for him just to pilot the ship through them without hitting anything. He eventually managed to weave his way past the debris, and discovered that it actually formed an enormous ring created by the gravity of the system's star. Within the ring was a single planet. It was covered in water, creating one huge ocean, which glinted in the star's golden light.

'I've never seen a planet like it,' said Black, gazing at its waters in wonder.

'In the tales of Earth, Poseidon was the god of the sea. It only makes sense that his planet is one vast ocean.' Tom ran the scanner, sweeping the planet for information. He was shocked when he found a result. 'The planet already has an entry in the ship's log. It's called Cronus, yet another link to ancient Earth mythology, it seems.'

'Entries like this were added to most Tsani ships. My people took the threat posed by other races very serious.'

'Not to inconvenience you both, but I don't see anywhere to land,' said Guard, interrupting them. 'Can this thing float?'

'I'd rather not try it.' Black shuffled in his chair. The thought of risking damage to his ship for any reason made him uneasy.

'We'll be fine,' said Tom, about the only thing had been sure of thus far. 'The ship is already designed to be airtight. If we activate the security bulkheads then that should hold back the pressure of the water.'

Black grumbled, not entirely convinced.

'Do it, just don't destroy my ship.'

Without hesitation, Tom threw the ship into a dive, soaring towards the planet. The *Roc's Feather* plummeted through the skies of Cronus, heading for its sky-blue seas. It hit the surface with an explosion of water, pushing into its murky depths.

The ocean teemed with the sea life of a thousand worlds. Among the sea horses and whales, Black recognised a blork, a species native to his world.

'It's like a huge zoo,' he noted. 'Some of these creatures are extinct on their home planets.'

Guard, having no time for sight-seeing, was only concerned with finishing their mission.

'Any idea where Poseidon is hiding, Tom?'

'The ocean is filled with life forms, so a bio-scan is out. I'll scan the seabed for technology.' He paused for a moment while he checked the results. 'There's some form of structure down there, it seems fairly large. Setting a course for it now.'

The *Roc's Feather* navigated through the dense waters. The sea life moved out of its way, intimidated by its size and shape. Their descent into the depths eventually revealed a huge castle, nestled safely at the bottom of the ocean.

'This looks like it,' said Tom, uneasily.

'Try find us a place to land. Do you think we can breathe down there?'

'The castle is encased in a protective bubble. It seems to be sealing in breathable air.'

'It looks like gods need to breathe too. Who knew?'

Tom settled the ship on one of the castle's high towers, and the crew readied themselves for what they would face outside.

Guard was the first one ready, and waited by the door to the bridge. Black cocked his pistol and joined Guard at the exit. The two of them looked to Tom, who was still putting on his armour at the helm.

'Tom, stay on board. I want us ready to leave in case things go south.'

'You got it,' he replied, rather pleased with the assignment. He never did want to go up against a god, anyway. 'Be careful out there.'

Watching them leave, he brought up the external cameras, following them as they wandered out into the mysterious castle.

Black stood on the ramparts and looked down at the area below. A lengthy Voltron ship was parked in the courtyard leading to the castle's main entrance. A chill ran down his spine when he gazed at the ship's sleek design. A splinter of a memory entered his mind, from a time he would rather forget.

'I recognise that ship,' he said, a distant look in his eyes.

'Is that a bad thing?' asked Guard, not used to seeing him act this way.
'I really hope not.'

He hopped off the rampart and walked away. Guard looked at him suspiciously. In times gone by he and Black shared everything with each other. He didn't like the idea of secrets being kept from him.

'Wait up! You're going to tell me whose ship that is.'

Black ignored him, choosing to enter the castle rather than answer him. Guard was never one to give up in any situation, and quickened his pace to catch up with his old friend.

'What's got you so rattled?'

'It's nothing,' he replied, rather unconvincingly.

With nothing further to say, he walked onwards, Guard following closely behind. They eventually reached a balcony, which overhung what appeared to be the castle's throne room.

From their heightened position, they could see Poseidon. In basic appearance he looked like a regular man; long grey beard and a well-toned body. What stood him apart from regular men was that he was twelve-foot tall, with a voice that boomed around his chamber. In one hand he held a huge trident, which had clearly seen battle in the past. While seated, he rested against the weapon, treating it like an old friend.

A Voltron entourage stood before the ancient god. Six Voltron flanked the hallway, standing behind a sole organic agent. Izak was clearly aware of his subordinates' limitations, and knew that a delicate touch was needed when negotiating with the deity. The agent was a Human female, one who Black recognised the moment he saw her.

Upon seeing the woman, Black was overcome by a sudden bout of insanity. He jumped from the balcony, splashing in the waters below. The whole meeting stopped due to his sudden interruption. The Voltron, their commander, and the deity, all turned their attention on him.

'What is the meaning of this interruption!' roared Poseidon. The whole room shook under the tremendous force of his voice. There was another splash of water and Guard joined his friend. The two of them froze, dominated by Poseidon's intense glare.

The Voltron agent was the first to speak. Behind her cold eyes shone a spark of warmth, as she recognised the sodden man before her.

'Captain Black.'

'It's nice to see you again, Katelyn. I see your time with the Voltron has been kind,' he said, indicating the small chunks of metal protruding from her face. Katelyn wanted to reply, but the dominant force in her mind stopped her from speaking further, reminding her of the purpose of her mission.

'I refuse to be ignored in my own chamber!' Poseidon slammed his trident on the ground. The resulting tremor made everyone in the room stumble, holding onto each other for support.

'Poseidon,' Black began, mustering confidence from some unknown fountain of willpower in his soul. 'It is an honour to meet you. Tales of your exploits can be heard far across the stars.'

'Flattery is a fool's device, mortal. Explain your presence here before me.'

'I come here to warn you of the purpose of your guests here.' He gestured to Katelyn and her Voltron companions.

'My guests offer the prospect of an alliance.' Black couldn't help but notice the sly look in Poseidon's eye as he spoke. 'Are you here to tell me that I should not accept their offer?'

Katelyn stepped in, an impulsive move to prevent her mission from failure.

'My lord Poseidon, this man before you is a known criminal in the eyes of the Voltron Empire. His list of lies and deceits are numerous. He is a man whose opinion is not to be trusted.'

'If I recall correctly, Katelyn, you were the one who lied.' Black let out a cheeky smile when he saw her reaction: her left eye twitched and her cheeks turned red, an involuntary reaction she hadn't even realised she had made.

'Wait a minute, you and her...' Guard's jaw fell open as he realised why Black had behaved so strangely since their arrival. During his absence, his friend had experienced more than he realised.

'Under their creator's guidance, the Voltron have swept through this galaxy on a mission to wipe out all organic life,' Black explained, ignoring Guard's questions through fear of another outburst from Poseidon. 'Izak seeks to seize your power, to use it for his own ends. There will be no room for you in his plans once he has what he wants.'

'You presume that I, a being who has lived longer than the rise of both of your civilisations, cannot see past your pathetic motives.' He held up his colossal arms and gestured up to the grand magnificence of their surroundings. 'I built these grand halls to serve as my own domain. I am not one to be controlled by either of your peoples. If you truly do know me by reputation, then you know that I do not welcome trespassers.' The God of the Seas raised his trident above his head. 'I trust you saw the spacecraft above this world. Take solace in the fact that it will serve as your tomb.'

Guard grabbed Black by the arm, pulling him away from the angered deity.

'I think it's time we got out of here.'

Katelyn and her Voltron clearly thought the same, and also fled the throne room. They were near the exit when the trident slammed to the ground. A shockwave rippled across the floor, heading towards them at an alarming speed. Not built for speed, the Voltron dragged behind the three organics, and were caught in the blast. Their circuits fried and they flopped to the floor.

Black held up his arm and spoke into the communicator on his wrist. 'Tom, act lively. Things have gone downhill out here. We need immediate extraction.'

On board the *Roc's Feather*, Tom sat at the helm, anxiously waiting for the others to return. At first he hadn't minded being asked to remain behind, but as time went on, he wished that he too had joined them when meeting Poseidon. He hadn't felt like himself since they had entered the system. It wasn't like him to be fearful of anything, yet since losing Valermos, he had discovered that there were some fears he didn't even realise he had. The addition of Guard to the crew had been welcome, as he still struggled to get on with Black. He had however begun to feel like the outsider, making him wonder whether that was the true cause of his anxiety.

'Tom, act lively. Things have gone downhill out here. We need immediate extraction.'

He almost leapt from his chair. His body moved faster than his mind, and before he became aware of it, he had already got the ship in the air. As the craft rose above the castle's high tower, he caught glimpse of Poseidon, and all his fears returned. What made it even worse was the look in his eyes: pure anger.

He brought the ship into a sharp dive, hoping he wouldn't be too late before the God's true malice was unleashed.

Black, Guard and Katelyn were starting to tire as they heard the first signs of Poseidon moving behind them.

'Just like old times, right?'

Guard first believed that Black was talking to him. When the Voltron agent replied, he was left with a slight taste of jealousy in his mouth.

'Those memories are from a time before I truly pledged my allegiance to the Voltron, and are therefore irrelevant.'

'What did they do to you, Katelyn? You always hated me, but at least back then there was a bit more shouting involved.'

Katelyn looked at him. For a moment she had the urge to snap at him, but quickly regained her composure, her objectiveness returned. She spared a moment to wonder why the enemy agent had caused such an emotional response in her. The thought was cut short by Poseidon's trident again striking the ground. Water whipped up from all sides, showering them in waves.

127

'It's Tom,' said Guard, pointing up to the *Roc's Feather*. The ship descended through the skies towards them, offering hope from the certain doom that followed close behind.

'Katelyn, come with us,' said Black, holding out his hand. She stared at the hand, locked in some kind of internal conflict.

'I can't,' she said. 'He won't let me.' She clawed at her head like something under the surface was trying to break free.

The boarding ramp lowered as Tom steadied the ship for them to climb aboard. Guard was about to grab hold when Poseidon's trident stabbed at the ship. The ship lurched upwards, avoiding the blast. It continued to ascend, leaving the others to wonder why.

They turned their heads to see Poseidon staring up to the skies. He looked at the *Roc's Feather*, the fires of hell in his eyes. His attention had wandered from those on the planet, and rested solely on the ship fleeing his grasp. His gargantuan feet lifted off the floor and he soared after the escaping vessel.

'Tom better know what he's doing,' Black grumbled as he watched his precious craft fade into the waters above.

Tom saw Poseidon raise his trident and pulled the ship into a sharp rise before his blow landed. The deity had marked the ship as his prime target, and he planned on utilising that in order to save his friends. Leaving them behind in the castle, he drew the ship out of the bubble, through the calm waters of the planet's ocean, and out into space. Poseidon remained closely behind at all times, and Tom was fully aware that he was heading for the place where thousands of ships had ended up wrecked long before his own.

His mind worked fast as he wove the ship in and out of the old derelicts. Poseidon had no need of manoeuvring, and instead batted the broken ships aside with his trident. His need to end the pursuit increased as after every passing second, Poseidon was gaining on him. He checked the ship's armaments. The *Roc's Feather* was equipped with a full bank of torpedoes and two laser turrets. Even if all of these were deployed at once, he doubted it would buy him much time, let alone fell the God altogether.

Catching sight of something in the clusters of wreckage, Tom pushed the engines to their limit, propelling the ship forwards. Poseidon remained ever close behind, and raised his trident, taking aim at the lone ship.

With Poseidon now away from the planet, the pressure of escape lessened on those left behind. Katelyn; however, failed to let this calm her, and she headed for her ship resting in the courtyard beyond.

'Katelyn, wait!' Black called after her.

She paused for a moment, before once again moving onward. Her movement was laboured, like she was fighting whatever worked the strings of her body.

'You are an enemy of the Voltron. Be fortunate that I have not terminated you.'

'She seems enchanting,' said Guard, sarcastically. 'I totally understand what you see in her.'

They caught up to her and stood with her at the entrance to her ship.

'We're in the same boat here. Can we hitch a lift? We don't want to be hanging around when Poseidon comes back.'

'That is… unacceptable,' she said, as if forcing the words from her mouth.

'Well it's a good job we're not giving you a choice in the matter.' Guard threw a punch, catching the side of her face. She fell to the floor in an instant. For a moment Guard studied his fist, wondering if perhaps he had hit her a little too hard.

'Get the ship in the air,' said Black. 'I'll take care of her.'

'Just make sure you don't do anything else.'

Guard wandered into the ship, leaving him alone with Katelyn. He patted her gently, fearing what side of the woman would greet him when she woke.

Tom could see it: the Xiz saucer, drifting hopelessly among the wreckage of a thousand other ships. While he was sure all of them were good ships in their own right, only the saucer had what he wanted. His left hand drifted over to the scanner, and ran it on the alien ship. He hoped that the craft still had some power left. When the scan came back positive, he felt a flicker of hope shine inside of him. *Right, now all I need to do is see if I can spark a reaction in the weapon's chamber.*

He fired a single shot from the ship's laser cannon, though this shot wasn't intended to destroy. The shot struck an exhaust port on the edge of the disk, its energy dissipating down the funnel and into the ship. After a moment's pause, there was a spark in the centre of the disk that flickered intermittently. A few seconds later, the energy began to build, and Tom knew that he had little time before it discharged through the craft's main weapon.

'Black better not hate me for this,' he said as he rammed the *Roc's Feather* into the Xiz vessel. The impact caused the saucer to spin in just the right direction, timed perfectly with the build up of energy to fire a full discharge in Poseidon's direction.

The blast caught the bearded deity unawares, striking him directly in the chest. His screams were so loud that Tom could hear them through the hull of the *Roc's Feather*. He turned the ship to see Poseidon writhing in agony. He had a hole in his chest; green static crackled from it through to every corner of his body. The static ripped through every cell in his body, tearing him apart. Eventually Poseidon, ancient God of the stars, was reduced to little more than dust.

Tom threw a fist in the air, celebrating the victory he hadn't believed possible. His heart continued to beat like a drum solo, even after the danger had passed. After taking a moment to compose himself, he returned to the controls, taking the ship back towards the planet to pick up his friends.

Black stood over Katelyn as her eyes began to open. All the while he kept his pistol near, just in case her first words weren't pleasant. She smiled as her eyes focused on him, and he was happy to see the same person he remembered from all those years ago. As she came to realise where she was, she pulled away, crawling backwards along the floor.

'Katelyn…' He held out an arm to her.

'No, Black.' She cast the hand away, rising to her feet.

'Katelyn, it's alright, you're safe. I'm not here to harm you.'

She studied him carefully, regarding him up and down.

'I'm not sure what to believe anymore.'

'What happened to you? Back on the planet you weren't the person I used to know.'

She unconsciously scratched at her head, as if feeling for something beneath the skin.

'Working for the Voltron is no simple task,' she explained, continuing to paw at her scalp. 'They did something to me, some kind of procedure. I can't remember everything, like there's something in my head scrambling out the details, controlling my behaviour. I haven't been in control of my thoughts for a long time. Back on the planet I started to feel their control start to lift, like I was finally starting to wake up after a long sleep.'

'It looks to me like that punch from Guard helped.'

'Or waking up to see you,' she replied with a twinkle in her eye.

Black blushed, not knowing what to say. Something about Katelyn knocked him off guard; he couldn't quite place his finger on it. No one else made him feel that way, and he struggled to decide if that was a good thing.

'Sorry to interrupt you two romantics,' Guard said from behind them. He had clearly been watching for some time. 'Tom's just made contact.'

'Is he alright?'

'More than alright,' he replied, barely able to hold back his excitement. 'He's only gone and killed Poseidon.'

'Unbelievable,' said Black. 'That'll teach the next God to mess with the *Roc's Feather*.'

While Black was overwhelmed, Katelyn, on the other hand, seemed visibly taken aback by the news.

'It looks like you failed your mission, Agent,' Guard gloated, taking pleasure from her misfortune.

Katelyn's body language changed quite drastically. She hunched her shoulders, and her hands began to tremble.

'Katelyn, what's wrong?' Black took her hands in his to help steady them.

'He's right. With Poseidon dead my mission is over.'

'Hey,' said Guard, genuinely feeling guilty about causing her so much distress. 'I didn't mean to be so harsh. It's a good thing really, there's one less vengeful God out there.'

'You don't understand, I can't be seen to fail him again.'

'Izak doesn't control you, Katelyn. You're free to carve your own path in life.'

'Lord Izak has powers far beyond what you know.' Her voice once again sounded robotic, as though someone else spoke through her. It returned to normal as she continued to speak. 'I don't think I'll ever be rid of him.'

'You could come with us. Fight alongside us against the Voltron.'

'I can't stay with you, Black.' They shared a look, both knowing that there was another meaning to the sentence. 'I have to leave. I'm putting you all in danger if I stay.'

'Okay,' he said. The pain it brought him to say the word was unimaginable, and he knew it would be a long time before he would forgive himself for doing so. 'Once we dock with the *Roc's Feather* you can go your own way. We won't stop you.'

'Thank you, Black. It's for the best.'

She smiled at him, throwing all her willpower into stopping herself from giving in to her urges to stay. She turned from them and headed away, mainly to avoid betraying her feelings through her facial expressions.

Black watched her walk away, a cold stare in his eyes.

'You okay?'

'Nope.'

A long metal corridor connected the *Roc's Feather* to Katelyn's ship, and Tom was waiting with open arms to welcome his comrades home.

'We were wondering when you'd turn up,' said Guard, locking him in a strong embrace. 'Nice work on dropping the God. I don't think even I could pull that off.'

'Who's the girl?' he asked, motioning to Katelyn, who stood with Black just out of earshot.

'An old flame.' Guard walked over to them, pretending not to notice as they hinted that their conversation was private. 'Come on, love birds, we can't hang around here much longer. The Voltron will be crawling all over this area before we know it.'

'Are you sure you'll be alright?' Black asked her, paying little attention to Guard's interruption.

'I just have to stay on the move,' she said, sounding more composed that she had earlier. 'If I keep going, I'll lose them eventually.'

'Why not travel to Alliance space?' asked Tom. 'They'll always give sanctuary to those running from the Voltron.'

'I'm afraid I made enemies in the Alliance long before I joined the Voltron. It was part of the hazard of being a thief.'

'Aren't you full of surprises?' Guard said, impressed. 'Are you sure you don't want to stay?'

'We could use the help,' Tom added.

She paused for a moment, staring at Black, who she knew felt the same.

'I'm a liability if I stay with you, but if you want a shot at stopping Izak, I can give you some intel. Recently he's been transporting a number of prisoners to a holding facility on Pridon.'

'What's it all for?'

'I don't know what he's doing there, but I know that the last guy I shipped there was very important to his plans. Izak sent me to personally collect him. He was a Jovian; I think his name was Valermos.'

The three of them shared looks of confusion and surprise. While their reactions differed, all of them had one shared emotion, one of hope.

'When was this?' Black asked, eagerly.

'A few days ago, it was my last mission before Poseidon.'

'But we lost Valermos weeks ago...' Tom's face lit up as he quickly pieced together the timelines of events. 'That means he's alive!'

'He was the last time I saw him, yeah,' said Katelyn. 'Who is he, anyway? Izak seemed desperate to capture him.'

'He's someone we thought we'd lost some time ago. Thank you, Katelyn, maybe there is a chance to set things right.'

'I certainly hope so, Black,' she said with a smile. 'I'll see you around.' Black watched her walk away until she was out of sight. He sighed deeply, wondering if he would ever see her again.

'If it's meant to be, you'll see her again.'

'You're right,' he said, drinking in Tom's words like wine. He turned to him and Guard with a wide smile smeared over his face.

'Come on, guys, let's go find our friend.'

Chapter 19

When the door swung open, the pounding in Valermos' heart ceased. Stood on the other side was Power Defender. His armour was polished and shone in the harsh white light of the corridor. He had clearly received some form of treatment since he last saw him on the desert where he had created him.

'Power Defender, am I glad to see you.'

'Relief noted, master.' The robot stepped into the room and began to unfasten his restraints.

'How did you get here? There was only one ship on the planet and that was the one that brought me here.'

'That statement is correct, master. I stowed away on the ship as it took off by holding on to the outer hull.'

'You were there the whole time?' Valermos asked, feeling shocked and slightly betrayed. 'Why didn't you try to save me?'

'The Voltron had greater numbers, and their organic leader possessed enhancements that would have made any attempt at rescue challenging. Instead I followed your progress along the terrain, keeping a safe distance at all times so as not to arouse attention.'

'Didn't the Voltron try and stop you? This place must be crawling with them.'

'It appears I was built from the remains of a former Voltron construction. The Voltron in this complex are currently unaware of my existence, therefore their sensors are not calibrated to designate me as a threat.'

'So you walked right in.' He smiled, pleased that his decision to create the robot had been a wise one. It also helped to relieve his concerns that his programming wasn't haunted by a Voltron presence. Despite this, he still believed a fresh systems check would be a wise idea once they got to safety.

Now unshackled from his restraints, Valermos was able to flex his muscles for the first time in days. His limbs had remained in the same position for so long that they were painfully stiff. It would take some recovery before they were back to normal.

'Tell me about the complex. What can we expect out there?'

'This entire area appears to be one vast containment facility. Subjects contained here appear to possess some form of scientific purpose for the Voltron.'

'Yeah I'd found that part out for myself,' he said, grimly recalling the reason Izak had him imprisoned here in the facility. 'We need to leave, as quickly as possible. Izak wants to use my DNA to activate an ancient Jovian artefact. With it he plans to destroy Earth and the billions of people on it.'

He was thankful for Power Defender's logical programming, as he did not question this new information, and instead focused his thought processes into getting them to freedom.

They left the cell and stepped out into the corridor beyond. The room stretched out for what seemed like miles, each five metre space separated by a door, leading to another occupied cell.

'There must be thousands of people held here,' said Valermos, a little shocked at the size of the place.

'Five thousand eight hundred and ninety-three,' Power Defender corrected him.

'We have to free them. Who knows what he has planned once he's done with them.'

'I do not believe that is a sensible course of action, Master. As you have said, the weapon Izak plans to unleash will kill billions people on Earth alone. If you were to be captured during the liberation the death count would be far higher.'

'I suppose you're right,' said Valermos, though the choice didn't sit well with him. 'Where do we need to go?'

'There is a shuttle bay not far from our present location. That holds our highest probability of escape.'

'Let's get moving.' Valermos followed his robot guide through the weaving corridors to the shuttle bay, at all times trying to take his mind off the helpless souls he was leaving behind.

It wasn't long after they entered the shuttle bay that their escape became known to the Voltron populating the area. A fire fight had ensued, and Valermos, with no weapon, had no option but to cower behind anything he could find while Power Defender fought off their attackers.

He found a nearby shuttle, and dove in and out of cover three times before he was able to unlock the door. Covering his head in his hands, he dashed inside. The pain in his arms was still intense, but the surge of adrenaline coursing through his body kept it at bay for the time being.

'Power Defender, in here!' he called. The drumming sound on the hull of the ship told him that the robot had heard him, as the Voltron shifted their aim towards it. Once the robot was inside, Valermos sealed the doors, and began the ignition sequence.

'The Voltron are attempting to seal us in.' Power Defender pointed to the shuttle bay doors, which were starting to close.

'Does this thing come with weapons?'

'Two laser cannons on the aft side,' the robot answered, at the same time calculating his master's next actions in his mind. 'You plan to blast through them?'

'I do,' Valermos said simply, bringing the ship into the air, heading for the doors.

'Aim for the section above the door. The plating will be weaker there.' Following Power Defender's advice, he targeted the ceiling just above the closing doors and fired. The shots connected and the roof came down, blocking the doors from fully closing. With just enough space, he guided the ship through the gap, and soared up into the upper atmosphere and into space.

'Good advice, Power Defender, we make quite the team.'

'I dedicate my subroutines to aid my support of others,' the robot replied. *He still needs some work with conversations*, Valermos thought with a smile on his lips.

He was surprised at the speed of their escape, and was pleased that it meant no Voltron were able to follow them directly from the base.

'Still no sign of pursuit?' he asked his co-pilot, trusting that his second opinion would appease his nerves.

'No Voltron ships have managed to leave the facility following our escape. It is likely that the doors were able to close, and the falling debris prevented them from being reopened.'

'Monitor all transmissions in the area, just in case. If there are any, it should give us a head's up of where they are and where they're headed.'

Power Defender's fingers swarmed over the keys, typing in commands quicker than his eyes could take in.

'The scan has picked up two Voltron craft in the system. Their scattered flight path suggests that they have adopted a search pattern.'

'I'll take us close to the star; the solar radiation should mask our signal.' Valermos reached over to adjust their course, and felt another sharp pain pass through his arm. He withdrew his arm and yelped in pain. The after-effects of the torture were still present, whether he tried to hide them or not.

'Master, I would advise that you take a brief rest from piloting the ship. I am perfectly capable of performing all the ship's functions on my own.'

He held his arm close and waited for the pain to subside. Even with the pressing problem of their escape, he knew he needed time to rest. *After all, who knows when the next fight will come?*

'Okay, Power Defender, you win.' He shifted from his seat and took the job of overseeing things from behind. The robot indeed was proficient at working the various stations. In some cases he didn't even need to look as his fingers manipulated the keys as though they had a life of their own.

Valermos was left with little to do than look over the readouts from the scanner. Something about the way the ships were moving seemed off to him, but he couldn't quite place it.

'Power Defender, something's not right with these readings. There's something unusual about their flight plan, but I can't quite place it.'

The droid took one quick glance at the scanner and left his multitasking mind to calculate the information while the rest of him worked on piloting the ship.

'It appears the Voltron are looking for someone else.'

The robot's words changed his whole perspective on the readouts. Valermos now realised that the Voltron ships were moving towards the facility. If they were hunting them, the ships would be moving *away* from it.

'Who could it be? We'd have picked another ship up on the scan if it was there.'

'Unknown; scans show that there are no habitable planets in the area.'

'Put your attention on it. If there's someone out there who needs our help then we're helping. It was bad enough leaving those prisoners behind.'

Power Defender complied, and patched himself into the communication systems. From there his operating system interfaced directly with the ship to detect patterns in the nearby area.

'The Voltron ships seem to be looking for the source of a distress signal.'

'Whoever is sending it must be crazy. Who sends out a distress call from right next to a Voltron stronghold?'

'Whoever the Voltron are searching for, they appear to possess intelligence far in advance of most races. The signal is sent by the manipulation of the sounds created by planets and stars. While the sound is audible to scanning systems, any attempt to trace its source would be automatically filtered out by the scanner as background radiation from the cosmos.'

'Can you pinpoint where it's coming from?'

'The addition of my AI to the computer allowed me to detect the signal. By working with the ship again I should be able to unravel the complexities of the code and reveal its origin.'

After a moment longer interfacing with the ship, Power Defender punched several buttons and flicked several switches. An image of the system's sun flashed up on one of the monitors.

'What does that mean?'

'It appears that the signal originates from the star's photosphere.'

Valermos checked over the droid's workings, but the same image of the star appeared on the screen.

'Bring us in closer.'

The ship juddered as it moved towards the red star at the heart of the system. He kept his eyes fixed on the sun's surface, unable to break his gaze. It felt as though something in the heart of the star was calling out to him, whispering its secrets.

'They're living on the surface.' he muttered under his breath, so quiet he hadn't even realised he'd said anything.

'Stars have no surface, Master. They are a collection of chemical reactions. If a being were to move too close to the surface it would be destroyed within seconds.'

'Why is it so impossible? Back on the *Roc's Feather* we encountered a race called the Helicron. They had the technology to harvest energy from a star. It's not much of a jump to assume that there is a race out there that can *live* on a star. After all, what better place is there to hide from the Voltron?'

'The possibility of such a species existing in the universe with this technology is possible, yet we have no logical basis for this course of action. The conclusion you have suggested is therefore improbable.'

'It just feels like the sun is talking to me. It's like something is calling out to me and begging me for help.'

'It is known that Jovians do possess a form of limited telepathy. The ability is more present in some members of the species than others. Do you recall any such displays of the ability in your past?'

A spark of memory flashed into Valermos' head: A girl, long locks of black hair. Was she a friend? The image disappeared just as quickly as it had appeared, leaving him once again focused on the mysterious signal from the star.

'Not that I can remember,' he replied. 'Perhaps they were just latent until something came along to spark them. It must be some kind of message I'm receiving from them.'

'Your present thoughts appear to come from a place far removed from logic. I suggest you look at this situation again from another perspective.'

'We have to land on the star,' he said, ignoring Power Defender completely.

'My prime directive is to protect you, Master. I cannot allow such an action to proceed.'

'You will if I order it,' he countered, developing a sudden attitude.

'While your logic is sound, Master, I still feel the need to protest. This action, should you be wrong, will end in your demise.'

Valermos continued to ignore the robot's valid concerns, and solely focused his attention on the star.

'Carry out a more detailed scan. There's something there, I just know it.'

Power Defender did as he was told. The results shocked the robot, forcing him to run the scan several times before he reported it to Valermos.

'What is it?' Valermos asked, excitement building within him.

'There's a small patch on the surface that is immensely cooler than the rest of the star. It may be theoretically possible to land on it.'

'I knew it!' the Jovian exclaimed, fist-pumping the air. 'Bring us down, shields on maximum.'

Landing on the surface of the star had been a surprisingly simple exercise. An odd cold spot existed around the landing site, and made their approach safer than they first thought.

Valermos was eager to leave the ship the moment they landed. The prospect of meeting an advanced species was too much for him to contain. He moved over to the exit and heard Power Defender's cautious voice behind him.

'Releasing the blast doors next to a sun would be very unwise. The light could leave you permanently blind.'

'I don't think so, Power Defender,' he said, pulling the lever.

With the blast doors down, Valermos wasn't surprised when he could safely perceive the majestic view that was the surface of the star. The blinding lights were safely filtered by a shaded material that covered the star's surface. He suspected that this was also how the beings they had tracked here were able to walk upon the photosphere. Closing one eye, he placed one foot forward and planted it on the surface. He was pleasantly surprised when his feet – and the rest of him – didn't burn upon contact.

'It looks like you were wrong about this place, Power Defender.'

'Your assessment seems correct, Master.' The robot followed him out of the ship and began scanning his immediate surroundings.

'The readings that I am receiving are illogical. Ending scan to avoid feedback error.'

'It's okay, Power Defender. Maybe this trip is a little outside your comfort zone.'

The robot's head jerked abruptly, sensing something nearby. 'Movement detected.'

Valermos' stomach lurched. He turned and saw three dark figures approaching. As the shapes grew closer, he found that his eyes couldn't properly focus on them. The figures continued to remain blurry and indistinct, even when they were right in front of him.

'Who are you?' he asked. Looking at the creatures for a prolonged period made his brain start to hurt.

142

'We are the Akranites. I am their leader, Lon.'

'It's truly an honour. My name is Valermos, a Jovian from Jupiter,' he said with sad eyes.

'We know your people of old, in the days when the stars would call out to each other in eternal delight. It is with deep regret that we hear that Jupiter sings no more.'

He was shocked that they knew of Jupiter's demise. He then remembered that the Akranites were telepathic, and the horror of losing his people was never far from his thoughts.

'My friend and I are fleeing the Voltron. They destroyed my world.'

He looked to check on his robot companion, who had remained silent thus far.

'Are you okay, Power Defender?'

'I appear unable to converse with these life forms. It seems that your words are also being broadcast through your thoughts, allowing you to converse with these beings through your telepathic abilities.'

'Okay, just try your best to keep up.'

Valermos had never known Power Defender to be inadequate, but he had to admit that he liked the feeling of superiority. He was conscious that he didn't want it to become a regular occurrence. Once they left this place, he was sure the status quo would return.

He turned back to the Akranites, who continued to shift blurrily outside his perception.

'So this is your technology; the way we are able to walk on this star?'

He pointed to the blazing inferno going on a hair's-breadth away from his feet.

'We unlocked the secrets of the cosmos when our race was young. While you looked to machinery in order to advance, we permeate matter itself. Our technology allows for us to reshape reality to suit our purposes. In this case it allows us to hide from the Voltron.'

'You won't have to hide any longer. We can point you in the direction of the Earth Alliance. They oppose the Voltron, and will keep you safe.'

The creatures became agitated. Their forms wobbled and blurred, their shapes becoming more unfocused. 'We cannot leave this place. We still hear the call of the others.'

'What do you mean?' The Akranites were an unusual species, their behaviour impossible to read. He was confused as to whether there had been some mistranslation or some other meaning to their words.

'The others are trapped. The Voltron hold them, keep them from us.'

'We thought you were reaching out for help. Your message sounded like a distress call to our ship.'

'The Voltron are no threat to us here. The star keeps us safe. We call to the others, reach out to them. Our song calls to them across the vast distance and soothes them in their captivity.'

The moment Lon spoke the words, Valermos knew exactly where the other Akranites were being held. After all, he had only just escaped there himself.

'There's a prison on the other side of this system,' Valermos explained. 'It's where Power Defender and I came from. We escaped from there just a few hours ago.'

'It appears that the Akranites were among the others beings held at the facility,' added Power Defender, breaking his silence.

'The others suffer at the hands of the Voltron. Their experiments hurt them. We hear their cries all too often.'

'We need to go back there.'

Valermos knew what he had to do. This was his chance to put things right instead of running. Black may not have got things right back on the space station, but he was doing it for the right reasons. This was his turn to believe in something.

'Our escape from the facility was enacted to get you as far away from the Voltron as possible. I believe that going back there would be an unnecessary risk.'

'I wasn't happy about leaving those prisoners there in the first place.' He refused to back down, knowing it was the right thing to do. 'Who knows what Izak has planned for those other prisoners? For all we know they could be the test subjects for weapons far more powerful than the one he needs me for.'

The Akranites watched them argue. Despite them bearing no similarities to his kind, Valermos could feel the love they had for their lost kindred. He refused to let anyone else lose their family the way he had lost his.

'Power Defender, board the ship and prepare for takeoff. We'll free those prisoners or die trying. Someone has to stand up to Izak, and it looks like it's going to be me.'

The Akranites watched the ship leave their safe haven. Through the telepathic link to their kind in the prison facility, they told them that help was on its way. The last Jovian was coming for them, and all Voltron should fear him.

Chapter 20

Valermos' return to the prison had been less fraught with danger than he'd anticipated. With Voltron seeking them at the fringes of the system, their ship slipped under the radar, landing safely in the facility. The ship touched down at the edge of the hanger to avoid detection, a trick Valermos had learned back on the space station.

A huge cleanup operation was underway in the area where, just hours before, he and Power Defender had made their initial escape from the facility. Huge cranes carried girders and supports to repair the hole in the hanger's ceiling. With the mess of the repairs taking up most of their processing, the Voltron were blissfully unaware that their enemy had broken into their base.

Valermos travelled through the corridors with a ruthless determination. He thought back to how he was when he first set out from Jupiter, and was proud when he realised how far he had come. In the early days he would have been terrified to even step onto a planet where he knew there were Voltron. The realisation came to him that by choosing to act, he could save the lives of those who were incapable of doing so themselves. That choice came as second nature to him, and he felt he had finally found his place in the universe.

They reached the cells, and found that the prisoners were rowdy, shouting and bawling at their captors. The Voltron had them lined up outside their cells, forcing them to march single file to another part of the facility.

'Where do you think they're taking them, Power Defender?'

'After your imprisonment you informed me that all the prisoners here served some role in Izak's campaign. Perhaps the prisoners are now about to fulfil that purpose.'

'Or they've already fulfilled that purpose,' he suggested, a grim look in his eyes.

'You propose that these prisoners are to be disposed of?'

'It sounds like what the Voltron would do. No matter what it is they're doing, it can't be good. We need to find out what's really going on and put a stop to it before these people get caught in the crossfire.'

'What are your orders, Master?'

Valermos raised his pistol and smiled.

'Follow my lead.'

He kept his weapon trained on the Voltron and slowly edged closer. There was little cover to hide behind, so it wasn't long before they were detected. Valermos fired upon the closest Voltron, watching it fall next to a bedazzled prisoner.

An exchange of blasts rocked the corridor. Valermos was pleased that he had reduced the gap between the two sides. His aim was still unrefined, and he feared hitting one of the prisoners. Power Defender was his greatest asset, his aim clinical in its precision. Voltron dropped all around with just a short burst from his rifle.

When the fight broke out, Valermos and Power Defender stood alone against their enemy. As the fighting continued, the prisoners began to take arms, looting weapons from the fallen Voltron. With their help, the tide of the battle turned very quickly. Before long the Voltron were overcome, lying broken at their feet.

No longer in danger, the prisoners turned to the one who had freed them. They began to cheer, revering the Jovian as a modern day hero. Valermos, not one for attention, played down their chants, preferring to stick to the task at hand.

'What are the Voltron doing with the prisoners?' he asked a stick-thin Human who struggled to heft the rifle he carried.

'They're working for a general named Rachak. He's rounding us all up, emptying every cell. I think they're planning to wipe us out. It looks like we've outlived our usefulness.'

'To the Voltron, perhaps,' he said in an inspiring tone. 'The universe, on the other hand, isn't quite done with you just yet.'

He looked to Power Defender, who kept a watchful gaze over the prisoners, keeping an eye out for any Voltron.

'I still haven't seen any Akranites,' he said to the robot, examining the crowd around them.

'We have only freed a fraction of the inmates this facility holds. It is reasonable to assume the Akranites are being held elsewhere.'

Valermos scratched his chin. He had promised the Akranites that he would free the members of their race imprisoned here. With this Voltron general rumoured to be culling the inmates, he feared that he was already too late. He took a leaf from Black's book, and decided to cut off the head of the beast, the one sure way of ending what was happening here.

'Power Defender, work on a way to free the other prisoners. I'm going to confront this general myself.'

'I believe this course of action to be reckless, Master. I should accompany you.'

'These people need someone to lead them. That person is you. Besides, it'll be good for your development.'

The robot stood, impassive. His purpose was to protect his master, but neither could he disregard his direct order.

'Affirmative, Master, the prisoners will be safe under my protection.'

With that, Valermos left his faithful companion, heading away from the cells towards the centre of the complex.

Valermos was able to navigate the inner regions of the facility with relative ease. In addition to the bland colour scheme, the pathways and rooms spared little room for complexity or imaginative thought. Every corridor was clearly labelled, and each intersection contained directions to all major operation centres of the facility.

While he felt compelled to visit the laboratories, he knew the detour would detract from the purpose of his mission. He followed the signs for the control centre, deducing that it would be the most likely place for a Voltron officer to inhabit. On the approach to the room's large double-doors, a familiar voice crept into his head, one he had successfully managed to ignore for some time.

What the hell are you doing?

He quashed the voice with the sum total of his willpower. He wouldn't let his doubts hold him back any longer. He had grown immeasurably as a person since seeing his world destroyed, and he wasn't about to let it all stand for nothing.

The doors reacted to his presence and swung open with a loud swish. The control centre was a large hub of computers and monitors. At the back of the room stood the General, who watched over the entire facility through the monitors' security feeds. Valermos spied three Voltron in the room as he entered, dispatching them quickly with a series of shots to the head.

The commotion made the General turn to face him. He winced as he saw clear wires pumping blue liquid to his metal jaw. Every part of the man's body had been replaced by Voltron components. The only former piece of the General that remained was his right arm, though even that was held in a metal frame. The General looked to Valermos more a puppet than a man.

'Valermos,' Rachak rasped. 'Lord Izak informed me you had escaped.'

'You'll find Izak is wrong about a great number of things.'

The General became visibly uncomfortable by the insult to his leader. 'When your Alliance burns to the ground, you will see who is wrong.'

Valermos wondered how someone could become so warped to believe in Izak's aims. Just looking at Rachak's appearance gave him that answer: you can make a person believe anything if you take away all that makes them Human.

'You're referring to the super weapon, right? Last time I checked, he needs me to operate it for him. It doesn't take a neurotic general to tell you that I won't be doing anything for Izak.'

'Your use to Lord Izak has ended,' said Rachak, his electronic voice sounding somewhat smug. 'He has found another way to power his weapon. It is preparing for departure as we speak. It will not be long before Earth falls to us.'

Valermos couldn't believe what he was hearing. He assumed that Earth would be safe if the Voltron failed to capture him. Not for a moment did he think that he would find a way for the weapon to work without him. All his life he believed his people's technology to be impregnable. That mistake stood as a chilling metaphor for how out of touch they were with the wider universe, a mistake that ultimately led to their destruction. Now he had made the same error, and he had no idea how to set things right again.

'With the weapon ready, Lord Izak no longer has need for the organics held here. I have been tasked with exterminating each and every one of the prisoners. Before long, no one will ever know that this place existed, including you.'

Rachak brandished a compact laser pistol from his exoskeleton. Valermos fell to the floor before the General had chance to take aim, hidden behind a tall computer bank. Sparks erupted as Rachak fired at him in a deranged frenzy. He refused to stop firing, and Valermos knew it wouldn't be long before his weapon needed time to recharge.

He dived behind another set of computers, and was able to get a quick bearing on Rachak's position in the room. More shots peppered the desk behind him, and Valermos waited patiently for the moment to strike.

As expected, the firing stopped. He leapt up from behind the desk, his finger ready on the trigger. As his head rose above cover, he was shocked to find Rachak there waiting for him. A metal hand grabbed his neck, holding him aloft in an amazing feat of strength. Valermos gasped for air, bringing his hands up instinctively to try and clear his blocked windpipe. His hand still clutching his pistol, he squeezed the trigger as the pressure on his throat increased. He didn't see where the shot landed, but knew it hit home when he was dropped to the floor. He wheezed as he sucked in air, struggling to take in breath. His bloodshot eyes looked upward to see Rachak screaming, his metallic jaw hanging loose on one side. He felt for his gun, realising it had fallen from his grasp some point after the shot was fired. As he crawled around, he saw the gun in front of him, round about the same time as Rachak.

The two of them shared a crazed look as they both realised that whoever used it would be the one to end the fight. Valermos crawled and Rachak stumbled, both ruthless in their determination to reach the weapon. Ultimately it was Valermos whose hand grasped the weapon first. He brought it to bear at point blank range, hammering a hailstorm of shots into the General's exposed abdomen.

Rachak lived long enough to see the light shine through the holes in his chest. After that, the lights in his eyes went cold and his body crashed to the floor.

Valermos rolled onto his back, taking in the victory that was his alone to celebrate. When the aching in his neck returned to tolerable levels, he left the control centre to check the progress of the uprising for himself.

When he returned, Valermos found Power Defender at the head of a gang of prisoners, all carrying weapons and armour taken from their former captors. He was thrilled to see three Akranites among those freed, their blurred shapes leaving them overt yet indistinct in the crowd.

'Rachak is dead,' Valermos announced to all who could hear. 'The Voltron no longer have a hold here.'

The crowd burst into a great cheer, some even fired their weapons in celebration. Back on Jupiter, his father held the highest office, so Valermos had never felt like a leader. In this moment he had his finally had a taste of the life that was intended for him. While he wasn't sure leadership was for him, after all, he took a moment to appreciate the good he had done here. He only wished that Tom could see him now.

'You appear to have pressure marks on your neck,' said Power Defender, giving his bruises the onceover with his superior vision. 'I would advise seeking medical attention.'

He shook off the robot's concern, but appreciated the thought all the same.

'It's fine, Power Defender, honestly. I'm a Jovian; it'll have healed in a couple of hours.'

He looked to the crowd. They seemed anxious, as if waiting for something to happen. It wasn't long before he realised they were waiting for him. They expected him to say something to them, some choice words to inspire them for the future. His only inspiration came from the last few months, the only true life he had ever led. Deciding that was a good place to start, he spoke up. All eyes turned to him. This was his moment to shine.

'Before I returned here, I too was a prisoner. Izak took from me my home, my friends, and then my freedom. I was lucky enough to escape, to have the whole universe open up to me. I returned to give every person here that same opportunity. For the time being, the Voltron are gone from this world, but it won't be long before they return. I urge you all to leave now, take a ship and go, carve out your own path.' He paused for a moment, hoping this next part would stick in their minds the most. 'I do ask that you never forget about your experiences here, not to punish yourselves over, but to give you the strength to change things. If left unopposed the Voltron will one day create another world, just like this, and the cycle will start over again. Each one of you has it within you to rise up and make a stand. Don't let me down.'

The reaction from the crowd was mixed. Some looked scared, while others seemed to take on board what he said. One thing the people wholly agreed on was to make their way to the hanger to find a ship. The crowd dispersed, and Valermos was glad to see them go. Now they could be free, something he hadn't truly felt in a long time.

When the crowd had gone only three were left standing in its place. Valermos paid little attention to them at first, but something in his mind told him to look again. For a moment he thought he was dreaming. Stood before him were Tom and Black, accompanied by another he did not recognise.

'Looks like we're a little late to the party,' Black said, a warm smile on his face.

Valermos smiled brighter than he ever had in his life.

'You don't know the half of it.'

Katelyn stuck to the shadows, a wise move in her opinion. Shadows were difficult to find in this part of the galaxy. Very few settlements managed to thrive in Voltron-occupied space. Kloros was one such settlement, located at the very edge of established Voltron territory. She had worked out a plan in her head the moment she had departed from the *Roc's Feather*. It would take her two days to escape into Draxi space; there she would find some safety from the Voltron. The Draxi were an economic culture, whose whole existence thrived on the buying and selling of commodities. They wouldn't mind buying the odd bit of stolen merchandise, in fact, she was banking on it.

She had dumped her old ship at the first opportunity, selling it for a fraction of its worth to a Menith slaver named Tarrl. He was a pushy character, and that played in his favour. She had to sell it cheap; holding onto it any longer would only lead the Voltron to her. Who knew how many trackers they had placed there? Izak was never one to trust an organic.

Her liberation from the Voltron implants felt wondrous. She could hardly remember the last time she felt truly free. She had been so weak when she started working for the Voltron, so desperate for something to eat that she took the first offer she got. If only she knew then that her choice that day would have led to the life it did. Despite all that, Black had given her a second chance, a shot at starting out a new life, free of the Voltron. She had every intention of taking it.

The rain on Kloros was constant. She didn't mind, it helped her to stay hidden. She moved along the pavement with her hands in the deep pockets of her long coat. A light shone on her from a nearby sign. She looked up and read the words "Shuttle Station." Burying her head in her upturned collar, she walked inside, all the time trying to shift the feeling that she was being watched.

Hundreds of commuters filled the station, each following their own path as they filed onto the platforms. She scuffled through the masses to the ticket booth, where a Tauran stood behind a clear screen.

'What's your destination?' the Tauran asked with a gruff voice. Katelyn struggled to tell whether the gruffness was because he was rude, or if all his species sounded like that. She decided it was the former; she had never been one to judge a book by its cover. After all, no one ever guessed that she was a Voltron agent.

'Vega,' she replied, trying her best not to let her anger rise to the surface.

'That'll be three hundred credits.'

Three hundred credits was a little steep, even for a long haul flight, but she had no choice but to pay up. Her number one priority now was getting as far away from the Voltron as possible. No matter how much she needed to spend to achieve that aim, she would always be able to recoup her losses at a later date. She slid the credits across the counter and the Tauran accepted them with a grunt. In return, he gave her a white ticket with her destination written at the top in bold lettering. Without further conversation, she left the counter and headed for her shuttle platform. Her ticket informed her that the shuttle was embarking from platform three, just a short walk across the length of the station. That walk turned out to be one of the longest of her life: after each step, the feeling that she was being watched increased. Every other second she glanced over her shoulder, hoping she wouldn't make eye contact with someone skulking in the shadows, watching her from a distance.

When she arrived at the platform people were already boarding her shuttle. She wasted no time in joining them, searching for a seat out of the way. She sat in the corner of the passenger area next to a Venusian, who almost smothered her with its enormous size. She didn't mind this; however, as it only added to her concealment aboard the vessel.

The safety video began to play on the back of the seat in front of her. She ignored the majority of the advice, impatient to be up in the air. Anxious thoughts began to grow in her mind, and had increased in intensity now that she was so close to leaving the planet. All she wanted was to be free in a life under her control.

Those dreams were dashed when the video came to a sudden stop, long before the footage had ended. The passengers on the ship looked around in confusion. A Menith on the front row rose from his seat to question the interruption. He was told to remain seated by the shuttle's staff. It was at this point Katelyn realised that something serious was happening.

She rose to her feet and caught the attendant's attention almost immediately. Ignoring him as he made straight for her, she headed for the emergency exit. As she fumbled with the release catch, the attendant crept up behind her.

'I'm sorry, ma'am, no one is allowed to leave the shuttle at this time.' Katelyn rounded on the attendant, staring deep into his eyes with a crazed stare.

'And why aren't we allowed to leave?' she asked, not realising that she had raised her voice.

'We've been asked by Space Traffic Control to suspend all space travel for the foreseeable future. There's some issue with our airspace, so I've heard.'

They're here.

She shook the handle with all her strength, but it failed to budge. Feeling trapped and frustrated, she yanked the handle violently, much to the attendant's irritation.

'Please return to your seat. I'm sure everything will be sorted out in due course.'

'You don't understand. You have to let me out!'

'Please, ma'am, if you'll just take your-'

She rounded on the attendant, grasping him by the collar. He looked at her with wide eyes and his body went limp.

'I will not take my seat when there's a good chance that we're all going to die in this damn thing!'

Releasing the attendant, she drew her pistol and aimed it at the catch. A single shot knocked the mechanism clean off, and the door swung open. Ignoring the protestations from the alarmed attendant, she exited the vessel, jumping over twelve feet to ground level.

Flood lights shone down from the night sky, bathing the streets in a harsh white glow. Katelyn recognised the ships immediately, and her heart was gripped with fear.

Destruction reigned down from the Voltron ships, showering the planet's taller buildings in flame. She heard the sound of metal boots clanging in the distance, coupled with the screams of the dying.

Her heart raced as the feeling of entrapment remained, despite leaving the transport shuttle. Her first instinct was to seek cover from the spotlights. She spotted a dark alley which offered perfect protection from the light.

The only sound in the alley was the cacophony of rain, bouncing off paving and litter strewn across the ground. The noise of the dying could still be heard from the surrounding streets, growing closer with each passing moment. While the alley offered some sanctuary from the invaders, but she knew it wouldn't last.

There was a crash behind her, and before she was even conscious of it, she had spun round, aiming her pistol at the source of the noise. It was hard for her to see in the dark, but she could swear she saw something moving near a small bench. She crouched down and crawled towards the bench, her pistol trained on it at all times.

'Step out from behind the bench,' she said, softly. 'I have a gun.'

Something lunged at her from the shadows. She rolled backwards and fired into the air. She heard a screech and a cat emerged from beneath the bench and darted down the alley. She cursed to herself, feeling stupid for getting so worked up over nothing. In recent times, the implant in her head had controlled her emotions for her. Since its malfunction, it was taking some effort for her to regulate these feelings on her own. She took in shallow breaths in an effort to bring herself back under control.

'Do you feel scared, Agent?'

Katelyn jumped, startled. The voice came from behind her, and she struggled to bring herself to look. She recognised the metallic voice immediately, and knew her days of freedom were limited.

'I prefer to call it repulsed, Grenik.'

'I find fear a useless emotion. It distracts the mind, leaving you vulnerable.' Grenik chuckled. 'You appear exceptionally vulnerable to my eyes.'

'I'd say that it's fear that makes us feel alive. Not that you'd know anything about that.'

She failed to see Grenik in the shadows, for a moment wondering if she was imagining him. Regardless, he stood further into the alley, leaving the exit onto the street free for her to make an escape. She made for the exit, breaking into a run. Grenik's menacing giggling echoed around the alley, and her heart sank when she realised why. Before she made it to the street, three silhouettes blocked the way. From their outline she recognised them as Voltron, their flimsy limbs unlike any other being she had encountered.

'We were always going to find you, Agent Katelyn. You can never escape us, no matter how far you run.'

She scanned her surroundings, looking for any avenue of escape, no matter how difficult. Every time she came up empty. She wanted to run, truly she did, but with the Voltron closing in, she had no choice than to resort to extreme measures. She brought her pistol to bear, intending to fight her way to freedom. Before she was able to squeeze the trigger, a crippling pain shot through every nerve in her body, and the gun clattered to the floor, unused. Her body went into a spasm, and she doubled up, completely incapacitated.

'What have you done to me?' she asked, fighting against her compromised muscles to form the words in her mouth.

'Your implant performs much more functions than controlling your behaviour. The moment the device was damaged, a homing signal was activated in the implant, leading us straight to you. Luckily for us no matter how much you damage the implant, it will still allow me to release an electrical pulse.'

While her body twitched on the ground, the three Voltron set to work on her. Two of them surrounded her prone form, while the third knelt down beside her. It placed a blindfold over her eyes, and hoisted her up to her feet. All the while they carried her, Katelyn remained wide awake, yet completely paralyzed. She felt every knock and blow as she was dragged helplessly through the streets. Grenik's voice was the last thing she heard before she was stowed on board the Voltron ship.

'This time, Agent Katelyn, they'll be no escape from the Voltron.'

Tom couldn't believe the sight before him. Having just come to terms with his death, he found himself staring up at Valermos, large as life, just having freed a whole planet from the clutches of the Voltron. The man before him looked different, older, hardened by life on the frontier. Nevertheless, under the surface, he still saw the Jovian prince he had served for almost ten years.

Valermos ran towards them with open arms, a gesture Tom was more than willing to reciprocate. In that moment, any prospect of it being a dream vanished. His friend really had returned from the dead.

'Alright, you two, cut the bromance.' Black looked at the two of them with an uncomfortable look in his eyes.

'It's good to see you again, Black.' Valermos extended a hand to him.

'You too, Valermos,' he replied, shaking the hand with a firm grip.

'Is that all you have to say to him, Black?' said Tom, fixing him with a stern look.

Black looked at the floor. It was clear to see he wasn't used to confronting his emotions like this; nevertheless, he was willing to try.

'Look, Valermos, about the space station. I was desperate to put an end to things, but that shouldn't have meant-'

'Black, it's okay. The space station was a long time ago, for both of us. I think it's safe to say that all of us have changed since then. In the end, we all want to see Izak dead, so the next time we get a chance, we work together. Is that a deal?'

Black smiled. He liked this new Valermos.

'It's a deal.'

Guard coughed, feeling unloved with the lack of attention. With the attention shifting to him, he went to shake Valermos' hand.

'We haven't met,' he said. 'The name's Guard.'

Valermos smiled, turning to Black.

'You revived him!'

'It wasn't me, he woke up himself.'

'I heard you had a large part to play in that,' Guard continued. 'I thought I'd never get the chance to thank you.'

'Don't mention it. It's good to finally meet you. I thought you'd be bluer.'

'An unfortunate side effect of the revival,' he replied, glumly. 'The Human look is taking some getting used to.'

'What is that thing?' Black interrupted, pointing at Power Defender, one hand cautiously clutching his pistol.

'Don't worry, Black, there's nothing to worry about. His name is Power Defender, I created him from the Voltron assassin I fought back on the space station. Over the last few weeks he's become an invaluable asset, not to mention a friend.'

Despite the reassurances, Black continued to eye the robot suspiciously. It would take a long time for him to become accustomed to the idea of a friendly Voltron.

'We need to get moving,' said Guard. 'It won't be long before the Voltron come back here for answers.'

As the reunited crew walked into the hanger, Valermos was greeted by a sight he thought he'd never see again. The *Roc's Feather* stood in the centre of the hanger, dwarfing the other ships in both size and magnificence.

'I thought I'd never see her again,' he said, staring up at the ship as the others entered.

'It's good to have you back, old friend,' Tom said, patting him on the back before boarding the vessel with the others.

Valermos stepped inside the bridge, feeling at home the moment his foot made it across the threshold.

'Right, boys, get to your stations. I need us up in the air as soon as possible.'

He stepped towards the weapon's console to find Guard already occupying the post. Part of him couldn't help but feel he'd been replaced.

'I think I need a new post,' he said, sounding a little lost. There had been a lot of change since he was last on board the *Roc's Feather*.

'Take a seat at the helm with Tom,' Black said. 'We could use some help at tactical if we're going to find Izak.'

'I have something to share on that subject,' said Valermos, grimly recalling his time as a captive back on the facility.

'Go on,' Black replied, edging forward in his chair.

'It turns out that Izak has been hunting me ever since we left Jupiter. He wants me to operate a Jovian super weapon to destroy the Alliance.'

'This one's got quite the ego on him,' joked Guard. 'How do you know all this?'

'He captured me not long after I escaped the space station. I was held on the facility for a while until Power Defender freed me.'

'Where is this weapon now?' asked Tom. 'The Alliance needs to be warned immediately.'

'But if the weapon doesn't work without Valermos, why inform them at all.'

'That's the problem. The Voltron General running the facility told me Izak had found some way around having a Jovian operator. I don't think the weapon is ready for launch just yet, but we have to act quickly if we're going to stop him.'

'Izak could be hiding that weapon on one of a hundred worlds. We don't even know where to start.'

'I have one place we can start,' said Black, holding up a small device in his hand. 'I placed a tracker on Katelyn while she was unconscious. In the slim chance that the Voltron still have control over her, you can bet that's where she'll be.'

'Sounds a good place as any to start,' said Guard. 'Just remind me to lock my doors the next time I fall asleep.'

Black handed the tracker over to Valermos. He hooked the device up to the navigation console. A small planet appeared on the screen. The image zoomed out; displaying the star system the planet was located in.

'That's Voltron territory,' said Black. 'If Katelyn was in control of her own mind, she'd have put Voltron space far behind her by now.'

'The tracker hasn't pinged for a few hours now, but I'll set a course.' Tom inputted the coordinates into the helm.

'Let's just hope we're not too late.'

The ship adjusted its course, sending them hurtling through space at tremendous speed. They followed Katelyn's last known location to an unimpressive world, predominantly covered in grey. The plant life on the surface grew in strange patterns, as though affected by a strange disease. The rocks were similarly disfigured, mostly scorched and grazed by unknown means.

'What the hell happened here?' asked Tom.

'Looks like a test site,' proposed Guard. 'Those scorch marks look like they came from a weapon.'

'This has to be where they're holding the weapon.' Valermos scanned the planet for any trace of their target. 'I'm picking up Voltron architecture on the other side of the planet.'

'Take us there,' Black said to Tom, before turning back to Valermos. 'Run a scan for Jovian technology. See if you can locate the weapon.'

The scanner swept through the planet, fine-tuned to pick up something as small as a toothbrush, so long as it was manufactured by Jovian means. Valermos was disheartened when the results showed not even a single sign of the weapon, nor any other Jovian artefacts located anywhere on the planet.

'Nothing,' he informed Black, hitting the desk hard with his right hand.

'We're not giving up just yet. We'll just have to find someone down there who does know where it is.'

The Voltron construction was a city-sized satellite dish, smeared with the same scorch marks seen elsewhere on the planet. It was clear from the outset that many weapons had been tested in the area. Cannons and turrets hung from large cranes, waiting to be attached to Voltron craft. Large mounds of bone could be seen at mile intervals, the unfortunate subjects of former tests. The sights made Valermos feel sick, and he feared what the Jovian weapon could do if it was unleashed on the innocent.

As they walked the walkways above the various test areas, they were alarmed to find that the place was abandoned. Their voices echoed in the empty rooms; the whole area looking and feeling like a ghost town. 'The Voltron left here in a hurry,' said Black, picking a discarded rifle off the floor.

'Do you think the weapon was held here?' They had walked through many sites already, but none of them had come close to being sizable enough to house the weapon that Valermos had described.

'In all my years fighting the Voltron, I never even knew a place like this existed. If Izak held the weapon for any length of time, it had to be here.'

'But it's not here any longer, Black,' said Valermos, a sense of panic rising in him. 'Izak could already be on his way to Earth. The more time we spend here, the more lives we put in danger.'

'You're right, but what about Katelyn? The tracker said she'd been here. Even though the information is outdated, they might have left her behind. I won't leave here until I know where she is.'

'If you're here for Agent Katelyn, I'm afraid you've just missed her.' The five of them responded to the sound behind them, all aiming their weapons in its direction. The voice came from a stout alien hiding in the shadows. Despite the poor lighting, it was plain to see that he was almost entirely augmented by Voltron technology. Black almost felt sick to his stomach just looking at him.

'Das Grenik.' He spat the words from his lips, recognising the alien almost immediately. 'Your reputation precedes you.'

'As does yours, Captain Black, though I never thought we'd get the chance to meet.'

'I bet you've been dreading it,' Black replied, advancing towards him with a menacing look in his eyes.

'I wouldn't,' Grenik said, pushing a compact pistol into the light. 'I'm armed.'

Valermos nodded to Power Defender. The robot fired a single burst from his rifle, severing Grenik's hand at the wrist. He screamed as his weapon clattered to the floor, his hand still attached. Guard advanced on him, kicking away the severed appendage, and hoisting him up in the air.

'You're going to listen to me very carefully,' he said, squeezing at the pipes that pumped vital fluids into his organic systems. 'We're here for answers, and you're going to give them to us. It's up to you whether you give them to us willingly, but I advise you now, it will be a much easier option.'

The hideous hybrid stayed silent, his small legs kicking in the air. He had no power in this position, something he was becoming increasingly aware of.

'We came here looking for the Jovian weapon Izak is assembling,' said Black, his voice taking a deeper tone than usual. 'You're going to tell me where it is.'

'I have no knowledge of any weapon, Captain. My presence here is purely of a surgical nature.'

Grenik's translucent lips widened into a smile, and Black's patience began to grow increasingly thin. He nodded to Guard, who delivered a sharp blow to his stomach. Grenik doubled up into a ball, which hurt even more with the force of gravity pulling him down.

'I advise you start talking. No matter how many modifications you've made to your body, my pal Guard here's a strong guy. He could tear you in two if he wanted, and I'm quite sure he does.'

Grenik's face took on a sour tone, as he knew Black's words to be true. 'Izak left a few hours ago, taking the weapon with him.'

Valermos jumped in, a part of him feeling personally responsible for the weapon.

'How did he get it working, I thought he needed a live Jovian subject?'
'Some artefact he had Katelyn pick up a few weeks ago, it's Jovian in origin. He reverse engineered the technology and bypassed the weapon's control matrix. He has complete control over the weapon now.'
'Where is Katelyn,' asked Black. 'Is she alright?'
'She left when Izak did. You'll find her quite different when you meet her again; she's been quite the subject for my experiments.'
Grenik couldn't help but let slip a sly smile. He always had pride in his work, and Katelyn remained one of his best. That smile would prove to be a foolish mistake. Black's eyes glowed red, hot with revenge. He had Guard drop him, preferring to continue the work on his own.
'You're a pathetic little man, Grenik, a servant to a master who truly has no care whether you live or die. As you lie trapped here, bleeding to death, I hope you remember that.'
In addition to his severed hand, Black left him another wound. He raised his pistol and fired it at Grenik's leg. The metal implants erupted in a shower of shrapnel, and blue fluid leaked out across the floor. Black held no remorse as he left Grenik there, hopeless and alone. He took his friends and returned to the *Roc's Feather*, the urgency of their mission ever-present in his mind.

Minutes later, the *Roc's Feather* was in the air, soaring through the atmosphere at full speed. They broke into space moments later, feeling the inertia as he ordered Tom not to slow down for anything.
'How are we going to find them?' Tom asked. 'Izak could have taken any number of routes to Earth.'
'Out here in the depths of Voltron space we've always been alone,' explained Black. 'This time Izak is heading into our territory, where we have a lot more feet on the ground.'
'Opening the fleet-wide broadcast,' said Valermos.
Black nodded, rising from his chair to address his superiors on all frequencies.

'Calling all Alliance ships, this is Captain Black of the *Roc's Feather*. Izak has amassed a fleet and is on his way to Earth. He carries with him the means to wipe out entire planets, and he plans on making the heart of the Alliance his first target. The search for Izak is top priority; if he reaches Earth then the battle is lost. I wish you all the best of luck. See you on the other side.'

Valermos ceased transmitting, silently wishing the fleet the best of luck. Black looked stressed, the bags under his eyes were already heavy with the turmoil of the past few weeks.

'Sounds like this is going to be the brawl of a lifetime,' said Guard.

'This fight is going to push us all to the limits. We don't know when we're going to find this thing, so I suggest you all get ready now. Put on your best armour, and arm yourselves to the teeth. We're not going out without a fight.'

Admiral Moore cursed when he regained consciousness. His body was covered in the remains of his ceiling. The rubble rolled off him as he righted himself, one hand on his desk for support. His aging body ached, even more so after waking up. As he came round, his mind started to piece together what had happened.

The fleet, we're being attacked.

In a flash, the memories came flooding back to him: mere moments after receiving the communication from the *Roc's Feather*, the Voltron fleet had arrived. They came in overwhelming numbers, laying waste to everything in their path.

Moore ran to the window and looked out at his craft. The *Frontier*, the flagship of the Earth Alliance fleet was now a ruined heap of metal, drifting through the vast emptiness of neutral space. Though his ship was in ruins, the battle continued. The remaining ships putting up a valiant fight against the Voltron. He had a moment of pride for his men out there, refusing to give in. Many of them had lost friends and family to the Voltron, which gave them a vengeful advantage their robot foes would never possess.

Another blow knocked his ship, almost making him lose his balance. A drilling sound followed, and Moore knew from experience what was about to happen. He pulled a pistol from his desk drawer and ran outside.

The corridor beyond his office was lit with a menacing red hue: the ship-wide warning they were under attack. A group of soldiers ran towards him, so in the moment they almost failed to notice that they were about to pass their commanding officer.

'You men, come with me.'

The men stopped in their tracks at breakneck speed and snapped to attention.

'Yes sir. We were about to head to engineering and assist with repairs.'

'They'll be no use in engineering if we don't stop the Voltron first. That latest knock was the sound of a boarding drill striking the ship.'

'Why would the Voltron want to board, sir? We have nothing here of value to them.'

'On the contrary, my boy, boarding the flagship to kill a fleet's commanding officer is a standard Voltron tactic. A fleet with no leadership is vulnerable. It is because of this manoeuvre we lost the Battle of Troy, and that is a battle I will never forget.' He stroked the scar on his cheek, a stern reminder of his days as a young officer. 'What's your name, soldier?'

'Matthews, sir.'

'Come, Matthews, there is much work to be done if we're to save our fleet.'

As Moore and his squad of troops rounded the corridor to the bridge, his suspicions were confirmed. A platoon of Voltron had forced their way through the ship's hull, and flooded into the ship. A number of bridge officers had opened fire, and were locked in a fire fight to prevent them from entering the bridge. The arrival of Moore created a second front to the attack, and prevented them from spreading across the ship.

'Richards!' Moore shouted above the sound of the fighting to a red-haired man leading the defence of the bridge. 'Broadcast a ship-wide alert: all available personnel to the bridge. The Voltron cannot be allowed to take control of the ship.'

Richards saluted, and ran from his cover behind a chair into the bridge. Another officer instantly replaced him, taking cover and firing on the Voltron.

Laser shots zipped past in all directions, making it hard to take aim without the possibility of being hit. Despite this, the Voltron were ultimately caught in the crossfire of both sides, and as reinforcements arrived to support, an Alliance victory was inevitable. As both sides continued their assault on the trapped robots, their numbers eventually thinned into a number that was easily vanquished.

With the skirmish over, Moore stepped over the fallen Voltron with a feeling of accomplishment. When it came to his own fallen, however, his tone shifted as he spared a moment for those who were lost in the fighting.

Entering the bridge, each soldier saluted him with deep respect. Over the passing years, he had earned that respect, and they knew he wouldn't let them down without making the Voltron suffer for it. He assumed his post and straightened his back, feeling the muscles pull, as they were still strained from the initial assault on the ship.

'Report; give me status on the battle.'

A young officer at the helm spoke up.

'The Voltron fleet has torn through our numbers. The core fleet has taken the worst of the damage; it's our fledgling vessels that are keeping the battle going.' Harris was a new recruit, but nevertheless held the same steely determination as the others. Moore had hand-picked her for that very reason. He always chose the best for his crew.

'Take the *Frontier* back into the battle. We must rally our forces if we're going to turn the tide.' He turned to Richards at communications. 'Start a fleet-wide broadcast.'

Richards established a channel to all Alliance vessels in the area, and then turned back to him.

'Awaiting your voice to begin transmission, Admiral.'

Moore nodded, clearing his throat before speaking.

'Calling all ships in the fleet, this is Admiral Moore. The Voltron have attempted to demoralize us by destroying our forces from within. If they continue to attack is while we are separated then we are doomed to fall into their trap. I need all able craft to rally to the *Frontier* so that we can fight the enemy together, as one.'

A number of ready checks on Moore's console informed him that the fleet had received his message. Only a small number of the surviving ships had charted a course to the *Frontier*, suggesting that they were the only ones still capable of flight in the fleet.

'Sir, what about our communication from the *Roc's Feather*?' asked Harris. 'There's been no sign of the weapon. This whole battle could just be a distraction.'

'We can't think about that now, Lieutenant. At the moment we need to focus on defeating the Voltron and saving those stranded on our immobile ships.'

'Yes, Admiral; shall I deploy shuttles to evacuate the stranded crew?'

'Immediately, Lieutenant, signal to the fleet to cover their-'

Moore's attention was taken by a huge object that dominated his view of the battlefield. Its size was almost larger than the entire fleet, and drifted at speed through the area. It resembled the head of a drill in shape; spiralling grooves covered its surface, leading to a point at its base. Huge engines on top of the drill-like area provided its propulsion, and also housed a large dome for inhabitation.

'Admiral, what is it?' asked one of the crew.

Moore continued to gaze at the structure in wonder, an empty feeling in his gut.

'I believe, son, that it's the weapon Captain Black informed us about.'

All Voltron ships in the area broke off their attack, grouping around the structure in a protective formation. One Alliance craft, the *Zealous*, attempted to follow. Several of the Voltron ships broke formation, cutting the craft to pieces under a barrage of fire. After just a few moments, the weapon, and all trace of its presence, had gone.

'How quickly can we get all our ships ready for departure?'

The confused and distracted faces around the room gave no reply. Moore knew that this was no time for hesitation.

'Look lively, people. That weapon is on its way to Earth. We need all available ships to scramble together and chase that thing down immediately.'

Harris was the first to reply. Her objectiveness in the face of danger caught Moore's attention. He planned on fast tracking her promotion to captain if they got out of this in one piece.

'The *Excelsior* has almost repaired their engines, and the *Nomad* is reporting that their weapons are back online. Only the *Firestorm* and the *Intrepid* are left making crucial repairs. Once they're ready and we've collected the survivors from the other ships, we should be ready to leave in around sixteen hours.'

'We need to be quicker than that, Lieutenant. At the speed that weapon's going, it'll reach Earth long before then. Are there any word on our other fleets?'

'Admiral Baker went silent not long after our fleet was attacked; Admiral Valentine has informed Command that he has rounded up every ship in the Troy shipyards and is on his way to Earth. The rest of the Admiralty has so far remained silent.'

Moore looked out at the stars and whispered a silent prayer for his comrades.

'Let's hope they show up soon,' he said with a distant look in his eyes. 'Earth is going to need all the help it can get.'

The trail of devastation the crew witnessed in their desperate flight towards Earth was sickening. The obliterated remains of Alliance ships littered the space lanes in the hundreds of systems surrounding Earth. The signs were grim, and they already feared they were too late.

'Checking the long range scans,' said Valermos. 'I'm detecting a large number of ships in the next system. It looks like the weapon hasn't quite made it to Earth just yet.'

'Get ready, guys, this is it.'

Black was dressed head to toe in Alliance combat armour. The reinforced material clung tight to the skin, allowing for increased movement without sacrificing protection. The others wore similar gear, save for Valermos, who chose to wear the ceremonial armour he wore during his escape from Jupiter.

The ship entered the system amidst a huge conflict. The Alliance ships in the area were succumbing to the sheer size of the Voltron fleet. Millions of ships swarmed through the system, acting as a buffer for a huge structure that drifted through the area: the Jovian weapon.

'There it is.'

A strange sensation ran through Valermos' body when he saw the object, not dissimilar to when he encountered the Akranites.

'That thing's almost the size of a moon!' Tom exclaimed. 'The devastation something that size could cause...'

'We're not going to allow that thing to do anything.' Black cut short all chatter and took complete control of the room. 'We have travelled the length of this galaxy, facing things I never even thought possible. If anyone's going to stop this thing, it's us.'

'We need to find a way on board if we're going to do that. Any ideas?'

'Those ships are going to make it impossible to dock normally,' said Valermos, mulling over the image on the scanner. 'They purposely seem to congregate around the weapon's entrances.'

Black regarded the weapon with a cold stare, his hands grasping the arms of his chair in a tight grip.

'This ship is more advanced than anything the Voltron can throw at us. If we can't make it in the conventional way, then we'll just have to blow our way in.'

'I like the way you think,' said Guard. He activated the weapon console, bringing its systems ready for use. 'Our energy weapons are fully charged. Ready when you are, Captain.'

Black smiled. His crew meant business. Each of them had suffered some loss at the hands of the Voltron, and each was ready for some payback.

'Tom, take us on a collision course. Izak will soon know the *Roc's Feather* is here.'

The ship propelled itself like a dart towards the Jovian machine. Guard picked off several fighters that strayed in their path, clearing the way for their main attack.

'Get ready, Guard,' said Black as they neared the swarm surrounding the weapon.

'Believe me, I'm ready. I've been ready for this moment my whole life.' His finger hovered over the trigger, ready to push down at a moment's notice. A number of Voltron craft noticed their approach, and moved to intercept. Black knew that this was the moment to strike.

'Light 'em up.'

He cackled, maniacally, slamming his fist down on the trigger. A huge burst of energy left the ship, ploughing through the advancing horde. The enemy craft buckled under the force of the blast, crumpling into dust. The remaining Voltron vessels bore down on them in overwhelming numbers, but were unable to keep up with the small blue craft as it zipped past their line.

'We're through,' said Black, punching the air. 'Now to make our way inside.'

'The Voltron will catch up to us if we head towards the hanger.'
Valermos scratched his head, thinking of another way into the
construct. 'Why don't we blast our way through the side?'
'This just gets better and better,' said Guard, rubbing his hands in
delight. He slammed down the trigger again, and the energy weapon
hammered into the side of the machine. After a moment of pressure,
the blast tore into the hull, leaving a hole just large enough for the
Roc's Feather to fit through. Tom's entry was a little off, and the ship's
side smacked against the hull as it passed through the hole, sending it
spiralling out of control. It crashed through several walls, spinning
wildly, before finally settling against a large support.
'Is everyone alright?' Black's question was met with a mixture of
moans, none of them bad enough to warrant concern. The crash left
the crew dazed, but mostly unharmed. Valermos checked the damage
the moment he came to: all systems were in working order.
'The ship's taken a few scratches, but nothing major.'
Tom felt embarrassed. The *Roc's Feather* was like a child to Black, and
if that entry was just a little wider off the mark, he could have been
responsible for the ship's destruction.
'Sorry.' He lowered his head; sensing retribution was to come at any
moment.
'The ship is the last of my worries at the moment.' Black hopped off his
chair. 'Come on, we need to get moving.'
In a state of shock, Tom was the last to vacate his seat. He had vastly
underestimated Black's desire to defeat the Voltron, it was practically
his number one driving force.
As he followed the others from the ship, he began to wonder the limits
he would go to when fighting the Voltron. He concluded there was
nothing he wouldn't do if it meant saving a friend.
The interior of the Jovian machine was an ornate affair. The walls were
decorated in a light brown, not too dissimilar from baked clay. Drawn
on them were delicate carvings of a history Valermos and his people

had long since forgotten. It was very possible that this place was the last vestibule of Jovian culture.

'It reminds you of home, doesn't it?' Tom looked at him with sad eyes.

'I think about it all the time,' he replied without a moment's thought.

'Maybe if we stop Izak we can salvage this place somehow?'

Valermos shook his head. It was a price to high to pay for him.

'I know how it feels to lose my home; I won't let you lose yours. We do whatever it takes to stop Izak, even if it means destroying this place.'

'That's what I want to hear,' said Black, stopping to pass out his orders. 'Valermos, I need you to get this weapon offline. Whatever bypass Izak has made to this thing, I'm willing to bet that a Jovian presence might just be able to reverse it. No one else needs to die because of Izak's madness.'

'I won't let you down.' Valermos said firmly, knowing he would stop at nothing to save a world from Jupiter's fate.

'We better get going,' said Tom, knowing that each second they wasted brought the weapon closer to Earth. Valermos nodded, and turned to his robot companion.

'Come on, Power Defender.'

Black stepped in to object.

'I need Power Defender to come with me.'

'I thought you weren't keen on robots?'

'He demonstrated his usefulness back at the test site with Grenik. Besides, if I'm going up against Izak, I'm going to need a decent bodyguard.'

'And where does that leave me?' asked Guard, quite hurt not to be considered for the position.

'This thing has to be powered by something. If either of us fails at our end, at least we can blow the damn thing up.'

'That sounds like my kind of plan. I work better alone, anyway.'

'Look after yourself, buddy,' Black added, his tone becoming serious. 'I don't want to be putting you in that freezer again.'

'Neither do I, my friend. You can't kill anything from inside a box.' He gave a brief smile and was off, running into the distance.

'Good luck, you two. Be careful out there.' Black gave them a nervous smile, before he too parted ways with them.

'Let's get going,' said Tom, choosing another path among the machine's network of corridors. Valermos gulped, this was the endgame he had thought about ever since he watched his planet fall, and after all he had been through, he still wasn't sure he was ready. Nevertheless, he followed his ally further into the ship. Today wasn't the day for speculation. It was time to act.

Black and Power Defender sprinted down endless corridors, which seemed to stretch out forever. Black's lungs burned, but Power Defender held the same pace, his mechanical limbs not feeling the same strain as himself.

'Power Defender, you need to slow down,' he panted, the exhaustion too much to bear any longer. He stopped a moment to catch his breath. The robot took the brief stop as an opportunity to scan the immediate area.

'Can you pinpoint Izak's location?' Black asked the robot, who was about as adept at sharing his thoughts without prompting as he was.

'The layout of the weapon seems to suggest that Izak will be found somewhere on the top level. His psychological profile suggests that he would enjoy being able to view the destruction that the weapon will cause.'

'That sounds like him,' Black said, wondering if Izak had done the same when his world fell. 'Lead the way.'

They ran through yet more corridors, and Black got the peculiar sensation that they were ascending with each step. At the point where one corridor curved away into another, Power Defender paused and raised his rifle.

'Voltron approaching,' he announced, attentively awaiting them.

Black turned the corner to see a group of Voltron heading towards them. They raised their weapons the moment they saw the intruders. Power Defender was firing at the Voltron before they had chance to take aim. Black raised his pistol and helped him pick off the approaching Voltron one by one. The enemy had no cover to hide behind, and were boxed in by the narrow confines of the corridor. As a result, they used the only tactic available to them; charging towards their enemy in a suicidal fashion. Power Defender and Black used this to their advantage, and barraged them laser fire, until each Voltron was a broken heap of parts on the floor.

'The observation deck is this way,' said Power Defender the moment the enemy were defeated, sprinting off once more. While Black admired the robot's clinical efficiency, he wished he had some concept of the limitations of his companion. He trundled after him, sluggishly, hoping their destination wasn't much further.

Within a few minutes, they had arrived at their destination. A large black door stood before them, an oddity when compared to the soft brown walls that surrounded it. What struck Black as even more odd was that the door had no handle, nor any other indication of how to enter.

'How do we get in?'

Before the robot could reply, the door swung open. Katelyn stood inside to greet them, hands clasped behind her back. She was accompanied by six Voltron guards, each aiming their weapons at them.

'Welcome to my master's lair,' she said in a dull tone that held no emotion. 'You are now his prisoners.'

She fired a pair of small dots at Power Defender. Upon impact, the dots crackled with electricity, incapacitating the robot in a matter of seconds. As another company of Voltron closed in from behind, Black was left wondering why it wasn't Izak who greeted them at the door.

The architecture of the Jovian machine came as second nature to Valermos. When Tom struggled to navigate the winding corridors, he took charge. Some part of him could just feel the path he should take, a subconscious tour guide leading him on.

His guidance brought them straight to the control room. The door opened automatically the moment he drew close.

'It's like you're being given the welcome mat,' Tom noted.

'Let's hope it lasts.'

The control room shocked Valermos by how bare it was. The room was wide and open. At the back was a small pedestal, resting in front of a large window.

He found himself drawn to the pedestal. It reached out to him in a soft voice, and something inside him spoke back. He approached, and felt the sensation of something rummaging around in his head.

'My name is Valermos, I am the sole heir to the throne of Jupiter.' He felt the words leave his lips, though he had no control over saying them.

A holographic image appeared above the pedestal, which Valermos instantly recognised to be that of Earth.

'It must be the target Izak has programmed in,' said Tom, a sense of alarm in his voice. 'We have to turn it off, right away.'

'I'd rather you didn't,' said a voice from behind them, one they recognised all too well.

Izak, leader of the Voltron race, and mastermind behind this whole attack, stood at the back of the room, glaring at them.

With the fate of his world at stake, Tom wasted no time with talk. He charged at Izak, screaming at the top of his voice. The purple-faced monstrosity caught him with his metal hand, lifting him into the air with augmented arms. Izak tossed him aside as though he were an insect. He landed just outside the doors, which closed behind him soon after.

'Get back to the others!' Valermos shouted, hoping his friend could hear him beyond the door. He reached for his pistol, safely tucked away in the scales of his armour.

'Prince Valermos, I'm not here to fight,' said the Voltron leader, holding up his steely arms in a gesture of peace. 'I've been wanting to bring you to this place for a long time.'

'I know why you've wanted me here,' spat Valermos, his hatred for him plain to see. 'You must know by now that I have no intention of helping you.'

'Not even when you could save your own people?'

Valermos was left gobsmacked. He had no idea what Izak had meant, but he would be a fool not to ask.

'What are you talking about?'

'This whole place is one huge terraformer. With the slightest whim you could bring your people back in moments.'

He had not even considered that. In all the time he'd spent travelling, wanting revenge for his people, not for one moment had he thought that he might be able bring them back.

'I could see my father again.'

Izak smiled, seeing that the temptation was working.

'That is the choice you must make, Valermos. With this device you could save Jupiter, recreate the whole planet, just like it was. All you have to do is give the command.'

'But the people on Earth...'

'Irrelevant,' Izak snapped. 'Mere pawns in a much larger game.'

There was the choice, the impossible conundrum that he already knew the answer to. Not for a moment could he destroy Earth, putting millions through the pain that he had felt. For the rest of his days he would never allow another soul to feel that agony.

'The answer is no, Izak. Nothing will ever bring my people back, not even your lies.'

'Then this is the moment where your race will finally become extinct.'

Izak drew a large sword from a compartment in his leg, the shadow it cast sending darkness across the room. Valermos clutched his pistol tightly, preparing himself for a fight.

Katelyn had Black tied to a chair. His bonds were tight, exceedingly tight. As a former thief, she certainly knew how to tie someone up so they could never escape. On the floor beside him was Power Defender. The dots that had been fired at his chest continued to give regular bursts of electricity, keeping him docile.

'Katelyn, what are you doing here?' Black asked, showing more concern than anything else.

'After Cronus I was granted my final reward. I have proven myself as Lord Izak's most loyal subject.'

'But your mission at Cronus was a failure, Katelyn. You left there a free woman, the same wonderful, independent woman I once knew. You didn't have to fear ever being controlled again.'

Power Defender's head twitched. For a moment Black believed he was malfunctioning, until he noticed his gaze was solely fixed on Katelyn.

'I am detecting an implantation inside her head, Captain Black. The device is used to give the creator a controlling influence over the subject. The concept of free will is no longer allowed to exist in her mind. She is now a true tool of the Voltron.'

'Don't you see Katelyn; Izak didn't reward you for your loyalty, he *forced* loyalty upon you.'

She twitched, as some part of her mind took in the information, but not enough to make a sizeable impact.

'Izak is always there, he has always been there. One day you will see it too.'

'You don't have to stand with them, you can help us. We need you, Katelyn.'

'I have made my choice, Black. My future lies with Lord Izak. You and your allies don't stand a chance against his almighty power. It won't be long before you, like so many others, fall beneath his feet.' While it was Katelyn's lips that moved, Black couldn't help but feel it was someone else that worked the strings. The Voltron presence in her mind had returned, and this time it was here to stay. Black knew he could do no more for her. Despite how much he cared for her, she was an enemy now, and to survive he had to treat her that way.

'You do realise that we have got this far, Katelyn. My friends and I are now standing in the most ancient and sophisticated weapon this galaxy has ever seen. If those millions of Voltron ships outside failed to stand in our way, do you really think Izak can?'

'Enough,' she said, a slight hint of anger in her voice. 'You will insult my master no longer.'

She raised her pistol at his head. Black stared down the barrel, and noticed that behind her a small grate in the ceiling was shaking. Katelyn failed to notice, continuing to hold the pistol, caught in an internal battle over whether or not to pull the trigger.

The grate came loose and fell to the floor with an almighty crash. Katelyn spun around to see Tom swinging from the ceiling towards her. He kicked her in the face. As she stumbled backwards, Black stuck out his leg, causing her to trip. She hit her head on the floor, and mumbled to herself for a moment before falling unconscious.

'Good timing,' said Black, relieved to be safe.

'I have my moments.'

Tom helped untie Black, and removed the restraining circuits from Power Defender. Black flexed his wrists, feeling the blood return to his hands.

'Tom,' Black said, checking behind him to make sure he was alone. 'Where's Valermos?'

Tom's gaze fell, and Black feared the worst.

'Izak showed up when we reached the control room. We were separated...'

Black wasted no time, and gathered his confiscated weaponry from the floor.

'We need to get there, right away.'

Guard had been running through corridors for what seemed like hours, mercilessly killing any Voltron he encountered. Since his emergence from the stasis pod, his physical condition was far superior to any person or Voltron he had yet encountered. So far he hadn't had a chance to test his new limits. A super weapon swarming with Voltron provided him with that opportunity, and so far he hadn't squandered it.

He turned his head to see a group of Voltron converging on his position, raising their weapons to take a shot at him. He lifted his arms to reveal a pistol in each hand. Firing from both weapons at once, he rolled forwards, at the same time avoiding each shot that was sent in his direction. By the time he was back on his feet, each Voltron in the squad was dead on the floor.

He checked his watch. It had been over an hour since he had parted ways with the others, and so far he had received no indication that their plans had been successful. He had tried to wait as long as possible before carrying out his own part of the plan, but if he waited any longer he risked the weapon reaching Earth. Sensing his time running short, he set out into the bowels of the ship, hoping to encounter more Voltron on the way.

Black and his allies ran through the corridors of the weapon as fast as they could. Power Defender held Katelyn over one shoulder, her weight failing to encumber him as he kept pace with the others. They reached the doors to the control room, and found them locked.

'It's totally fused,' said Tom. 'I tried to get back in when we were separated, but Izak must have done something to the controls.'

Black tried keypad next to the door, but found that the buttons were unresponsive.

'I think it's a job for you, big guy.' Black patted Power Defender on the back, and the robot got to work.

With one gargantuan kick, the doors flew open, and all the attention in the room was drawn to the newcomers. Valermos lay still on the floor, injured but alive. Stood over him was Izak, his red eye illuminating his silhouette with demonic intent.

'The crew of the *Roc's Feather*, come to face me as their Alliance falls all around them.'

'If the Alliance does fall, you can be damn sure we'll take you with it.' Black approached the Voltron leader, his friends fanning out behind him on both sides.

'You're too late, Captain,' Izak said, raising his hands in triumphant grandeur. 'My weapon has reached Earth. In a few hours the whole planet will turn to ash. Soon every world in the Alliance will suffer the same fate, and all presence of it having ever existed will be gone.'

'You're getting way too ahead of yourself.' Tom raised his pistol. 'We're not done fighting yet.'

He fired a single shot that headed straight for the cyborg's head. Izak saw the shot coming, and came prepared. He cleaved the blast in two with one precise strike from his sword. The deflected shot instead fizzled out of existence on the wall behind.

'It looks like we do this the old fashioned way,' said Black, rubbing his hands together, ready for a knees-up.

Voltron engineers threw themselves at Guard as he made his way into the engine room. His heightened reflexes worked overtime as they helped him to dodge and deflect each attack, throwing back his own when he could. One Voltron threw a punch at his face, which he deftly avoided, returning the gesture by driving his fist through its torso. His hand came out the other side, causing wiring and circuits to spill onto the floor.

While he revelled in the triumph, another Voltron snuck up behind him, grabbing his arms and lifting him into the air. Two more Voltron joined in, delivering punches to his exposed chest. Guard spread his legs apart and slammed the two Voltron together, their bodies shattering on impact. He then pushed his arms outwards, trying to loosen the grip of the Voltron that held him. The increased leverage allowed him to swing himself to one side, shifting his balance, bringing himself and the Voltron to the floor. From this new vantage, Guard quickly delivered a kick to its torso, severing it from its legs.

He got to his feet and studied his surroundings. All around were the dismembered remains of over a dozen Voltron.

'Well that was fun,' he said to himself, wiping a droplet of blood from his lip.

The engine room was a large chamber, filled with huge vats that contained the weapon's age-old fuel source. The substance inside the vats was so archaic that Guard failed to even recognise it. Despite this, it didn't take him long to work out that the substance was flammable. He approached one of the vats and pushed his fists into it. A thin yellow liquid seeped out of the container, spilling onto the floor. Thinking of his own safety, he ran back towards the door before firing upon the liquid. The yellow substance ignited instantly and the flame crept towards the vat at an alarming rate. Guard stepped out of the room and sealed the door, moments before everything inside exploded.

Black stepped forward, preparing himself for the fight. He stared up at the menacing form of Izak, who stood over a foot taller than him, and tried not to feel intimidated. Before he or anyone else was able to lay a finger on Izak, Power Defender pushed them aside, deciding to take on the enemy himself. The robot sprinted towards Izak, building up momentum, a true force to be reckoned with. His effort to protect his friends ultimately fell short, as, just seconds from delivering a blow, Izak struck first. His fist slammed into the robot's chest, instantly breaking through his armour and causing him to deactivate.

'You turn my own agents against me?' Izak boomed angrily.

He strode towards Black, all anger and rage. As he began his approach, the entire base shook and all the lights in the room went out. All Black could see through the darkness was Izak's electronic eye as it scanned the room.

'You've ruined everything!' Izak called out from the darkness.

In the back of his mind Black knew that Guard had completed the task set out for him. Before he had time to celebrate the destruction of the weapon, he knew that he still had one more task to complete for himself.

The back-up lighting kicked in and he saw Izak dashing towards him, arms outstretched. He and Tom fired on the Voltron leader, frustrated that their shots merely bounced off his armoured hide.

Izak continued to close in on them. As a last resort Black slammed himself into Izak, hoping to accomplish what Power Defender could not. He instead hit Izak like a brick wall, and crippling pain shot through his body like a lightning storm.

Izak hefted Black off the ground by the top of his head and threw him at Tom. Tom was knocked out instantly, and fell to the floor. Black carried on going and crashed into the wall behind him.

From his new vantage he saw Katelyn's unconscious body sprawled across the floor where Power Defender had left her. Izak noticed where he was looking, and smiled when he saw his broken agent all helpless and alone.

'My dear, Katelyn, how many times must you fail me?' He walked over to her prone form and placed a foot over her head. As he raised the foot to crush her, he heard a voice call out from behind him.

'Don't you dare!' Black shouted at the top of his voice. Dark-blue blood trickled down the side of his face, and his cheeks were swollen. Nevertheless, he refused to give in. He forced himself up, using all his willpower to keep going.

'Don't you ever give up?' Izak snarled, taking his attention away from Katelyn.

'Not when you destroy everything I care about.' He looked to Katelyn sleeping peacefully on the floor, knowing he would do anything to save her.

'It's so fortunate that the dead are unable to care.'

Izak leaped across the room in an amazing feat of athleticism. He landed right in front of Black, and launched a punch square in his face. He watched Black stagger backwards, his face covered in more navy-coloured blood. His feet faltered, and he tripped, falling onto his back.

'Your meddling in my affairs finally ends.' Izak raised his foot once more, covering Black in its shadow. He saw the steel foot bear down on him and closed his eyes, expecting the pain to come at any moment. All he heard was gunfire, and the pain never came.

Izak roared as laser fire pummelled into his back. He turned to face his attacker, and saw Valermos dragging himself off the floor, gun in hand.

'Another who refuses to fall,' Izak grumbled as he marched over to him.

Valermos looked to his friends; the people who came to the rescue when his end was almost near, those who never gave up even though they were in way over their heads. As he struggled to stay upright, he knew what he needed to say.

'That's why we will always win.'

He fell to the floor the moment the words left his lips, knowing he could go on no longer. He felt the familiar call of sleep, poking at him from the realms beyond consciousness. All he could hear from the waking world was Izak's chaotic laughter, mocking him as his world was about to end.

'Surprise, dickweed!'

Izak turned to see the source of the latest interruption. When he did so, he found himself staring down the barrel of a gun. The last thing he saw was a bright flash as the weapon went off, right between his eyes. A cocktail of sparks, wires and blood spewed from the back of his head and the tyrant crumpled to the floor, dead.

Holding the weapon was Black, covered in bruises and drenched in blood. He fell to his knees, spitting yet more blood from his mouth. Suddenly all the world faded away, and he stood staring at the sight of his fallen foe. After all the years spent dreaming of this moment, it had finally come. He spared a thought to all who had fallen; the sacrifices that had been made to bring him to this moment, where finally, it had all been worth it.

At the edge of the system, the cavalry had arrived. Twelve Alliance battle cruisers rocketed past Pluto, headed straight for the Voltron armada.

Admiral Moore headed the charge, his scarred face lined with determination. The Voltron invaders flew out to greet the newcomers, clashing with them in a plethora of fireworks.

'Hold fast,' Moore said over the fleet channel. 'This is our home. If it takes my dying breath, it won't see it fall today.'

Behind the approaching Voltron ships, Moore could see the Jovian artefact, firing a beam of light through Earth's atmosphere. As he watched, the light flickered, and small explosions erupted from the base of the machine.

'It looks like Captain Black and his team have done it.'

Waves of relief washed over him as he knew a pivotal part of the battle was over. The only threat that remained were the Voltron ships closing in on them, but Moore had no reason to fear them any longer.

'Break through the Voltron line,' he ordered to the fleet. 'We're heading for the Jovian weapon. We can mop this lot up when we know our men are safe. First we make sure the *Roc's Feather* makes it out alive.'

Black managed to rouse his allies as the whole station began to shake around them. He knew he didn't have long if they were to make their escape. The doors swished open and Guard entered.

'What the hell have you been doing?' asked Black, a spatter of blood escaping his lips as he spoke.

'I've punched a hole in this place bigger than Tsan's moon,' he said, a rumble from somewhere below them acting to prove his point. 'Come on, we need to get out of here before this place goes up in smoke.'

Guard hefted Tom over his back and dragged the broken shell of Power Defender on the floor behind him. Black helped Valermos to his feet as the Jovian continued to drift in and out of consciousness. As they made for the exit Black stopped, looking around for something. 'Black, what is it?' Guard asked impatiently as Black continued to scan the room with his eyes.

'She's gone.'

'Who has?'

'Katelyn was right here,' he said. 'She'd been out cold for a while.'

'She's a resourceful girl; she'll find her way out.'

Guard wasn't prepared to wait a moment longer, and carried his two friends from the room. Reluctantly Black had to agree, but that didn't stop him from looking back, right up until the moment the doors slammed shut behind him.

Small explosions started all around them as they made their way back to the ship. Rubble and shrapnel was thrown all around, and they were lucky not to be hit as finally the *Roc's Feather* came into view. They climbed on board and Black darted ahead, rushing to the bridge to start their escape.

The *Roc's Feather* left the confines of the weapon amidst thick plumes of smoke. Black didn't know where he was taking the ship, but knew that any destination was preferable to the one they currently found themselves in. The ship was buffeted by explosions that continued to ripple throughout the structure, yet they continued on despite the disruption. He pushed the engines to their limit, and the ship burst through the side of the artefact, pushing beyond into the safety of space.

There to greet them was twelve heavy battleships. The largest one Black recognised immediately: the *Frontier*, Admiral Moore's flagship.

'Calling the *Roc's Feather*, this is Admiral Moore. Hand over your piloting to us. You're in safe hands.'

'Yes Admiral,' he replied, finding it hard to speak as his mouth began to swell. 'It's good to be home.'

189

In the years since his own planet fell, he never felt happy calling any place home again. As he watched the lights from the *Frontier* welcome them in, he realised that a new home had been here for him all along.

'Black, I've settled everyone into the medical bay,' called Guard's voice over the intercom. 'Everyone's alright, just a little worse for wear.'

'That's great news, Guard. I'll see you all soon.'

Black wanted nothing more than to see his friends, but the ache in his bones was more than enough excuse to take a little rest. Limping over to the captain's chair, he threw himself down. The cushioned padding felt like he was sitting on clouds. He didn't plan on leaving the spot for at least a few days.

'Homeward bound,' he said as he closed his eyes. The pain in his body throbbed away until finally he drifted into a long, deep sleep.

#0198 - 281117 - C0 - 210/148/0 - PB - DID2044499